"NO, BOYD, NO! WE'LL BE KILLED!"

But Claire's screams were in vain. Cohoon had aimed the weapon carefully. The gun fired. The bullet tore through the heart of the ferry's ancient cable. For a moment nothing happened; then the wounded strands began to separate and unravel, stretching unbelievably and parting with slow reluctance. . . .

The lurch as the cable gave way threw the two of them to the deck. Then, free for the first time in its long life, John Black's ferry seemed to hesitate for an instant before it began to slide down Mad River toward the first of the roaring rapids between here and the Ford.

No man, dead or alive, had ever made it to Yellow Ford.

Mad River

by Donald Hamilton

FAWCETT GOLD MEDAL • NEW YORK

A Fawcett Gold Medal Book

Published by Ballantine Books

Copyright © 1956 by Donald Hamilton

ISBN 0-449-12977-2

A shorter version of this work previously appeared in serial form in Collier's magazine.

Manufactured in the United States of America

First Fawcett Gold Medal Edition: February 1964
First Ballantine Books Edition: February 1984
Ninth Printing: February 1989

1

He awoke at the bridge. The stage came to a full stop before venturing onto the long and narrow span. This, like the ore wagons they had passed along the road, was new to Boyd Cohoon. There had been no bridge here five years ago, and no one had written him of it.

He pushed his hat out of his eyes and sat up, leaning forward to look out the side window. Old John Black's cable was still in place, he saw, far below and a quarter mile downstream. Despite the afternoon shadows, he could make out the dizzy switchbacks of the old road cut into the canyon wall on either side. The ferry was tied up at the south landing, looking waterlogged and half-rotted already. The river swirled by it sullenly, yellow and creamy with sediment, the current gaining speed as it raced toward the narrow gorge below. Cohoon grimaced. Black's Ferry had become history in the time he had been away. He wondered how many other landmarks of his boyhood had changed or vanished.

A protesting movement beside him caused him to straighten up quickly. "I beg your pardon, ma'am."

The girl at his left said, "It's perfectly all right. Aside from a few broken ribs, I'm quite all right."

He had made his apology; he did not speak again. He wanted to look back at the land south of the river—it was strange that he could have slept, passing it—but he would have had to inconvenience the girl by the window again, and there was, after all, little to be seen from the road. From what had been written him, it seemed there was not much left to look at, anyway, except the land itself, and that would wait.

They were on solid ground now, climbing from the canyon's edge through the barren hills north of the river. Nothing had changed in here to amount to anything. There were some fresh rock slides, and once the driver stopped the stage and called down for someone to roll a large boulder out of the road, but that was the way it had always been along this stretch. As he and the man on his right responded to the call, Cohoon noted that neither of the two men in the opposite seat showed any inclination to help. They seemed disturbed by the halt, and moved apart to keep watch through the windows

5

on either side. Cohoon had already marked the pair because they were heavily armed and because they had taken the whole seat for themselves and the large valise they seemed to cherish, rather than give up the extra room to the lady in the company. It was a fairly transparent situation, and one, Cohoon reflected, that a man in his position would do well to ignore.

With the road clear again, they went on, following the same winding course as when he had been brought out this way in handcuffs five years ago. Perhaps the worst grades and curves had been somewhat gentled, but that was the extent of the change. They reached the top and started down through the clay hills; presently they were out on the flats. The dust and wind were worse out here. They always had been.

The girl riding beside Cohoon spoke again. "You act as if you'd been here before."

He hesitated, reluctant to be drawn into conversation. Then he said, "I was born here, ma'am."

She looked surprised. "Oh, I thought—"

She checked herself abruptly, and Cohoon saw that she was embarrassed. It was clear that she had taken stock of him early in the journey and classified him in her mind—by his unimpressive size, pale complexion, and by the cheap suit he was wearing—as not belonging to this country of large, tanned, and durably clad men.

He found her embarrassment uncomfortable, and spoke, therefore, as if he had not noticed it. "My mother taught the first English-speaking school in this part of Arizona. There was no bridge at that time, and the road, such as it was, came in over a pass to the west of the one we used today, and crossed at a ford thirty miles downstream." To converse with a woman, after the time that had passed, was a disconcerting experience. He forced himself to ask politely, "Are you acquainted with the Territory, ma'am?"

"No, I just know what I've been told. If I'd believed all of it, I'd have hesitated to make the trip." The girl smiled. "Maybe you can tell me the name of the river we just crossed."

"Well, the Mexicans had it named after some saint or other," Cohoon said, "but the Indians call it Crazy River or Mad River. It's kind of a tough crossing, most places, and I reckon a few savages got themselves drowned there from time to time."

"It looked as if there used to be a ferry of sorts down below the bridge."

6

"Yes," Cohoon said. Speech was coming more readily now. "That was Black's Ferry. Wasn't supposed to be too safe, in the old days."

The girl said, "It certainly didn't look safe."

"Oh, the ferry usually made it all right," Cohoon said. "But Old John Black was supposed to have a habit of shoving lone travelers over the side for whatever might be in their packs or saddlebags."

"Is that true," the girl demanded, turning quickly to look at him, "or is it just another story?"

Cohoon grinned. "Well, I used to know Willie Black, Old John's boy, but somehow I never did get around to asking him. We weren't exactly on friendly terms; my brother Jonathan shoved him overboard one day for a joke and he almost drowned before we got a rope on him and hauled him in. But certainly his dad never lacked money for hard liquor to the day of his death, although his family sometimes lacked food and clothing. On the other hand, no man who was swept down into the gorge ever climbed out to accuse him, nor did any bodies ever come out thirty miles below at Yellow Ford."

The girl shook her head. "Well, I was warned it was a wild country, full of heat and dust and dangerous men. Tell me, what were those mountains we went through south of the river? I hope you don't mind answering all these questions?"

"Not at all, ma'am. Those were the Candelaria Mountains, and the land lying between them and the river, west of the road, is the Candelaria Grant, formerly owned by a Spanish family of that name. It runs as far west as Yellow Ford."

"Thirty miles?" the girl said. "That's quite a bit of land, isn't it?"

"Not by local standards, ma'am," Cohoon said. "And some of it's pretty broken country. But it does include some of the prettiest grazing land in the Territory, although you wouldn't guess it by what you can see from the road. You have to come at it from the west to really . . ." He stopped, and cleared his throat. From talking too little, he was now coming to talk too much. It was hard to strike a proper balance, after five years. He went on, rather stiffly, "From the next rise, we ought to get a look at the Sombrero, if I remember rightly. It's kind of a local landmark. The town's a couple of miles this side of it, but hidden in a draw. There's the rock now." He pointed out the distant formation, a tremendous stone worn by wind and sand into a shape somewhat like that of a wide-brimmed hat, balanced upon a rock pinnacle over a hundred feet in height. After regarding it with interest, the girl raised her hands to her

7

hair as if to prepare herself for the entry into town. Cohoon grinned at this. "Distances out here are deceiving, ma'am," he said gently. "We have a good two hours yet."

The first thing he noted as they pulled into town was how greatly it had grown. Main Street was twice as long as it had been. There was a bank, a barbershop, a couple of new mercantile establishments, an assay office, and the office of some mining corporation, all housed in buildings that had a raw, new look. The town that Cohoon remembered had been characterized by the quiet colors of weathered boards and seasoned adobe: this town looked garish and unfriendly to him. The people, too, had changed. There were more of them —too many. They crowded the street and seemed in an unreasonable hurry. No one had ever hurried in the Sombrero he remembered.

The changes gave Cohoon an unpleasant sense of having been left behind by time, an old man at twenty-four. The stage came to a halt in front of the hotel, which had added a wing and a coat of paint since he had last seen it. He got out and helped the girl descend, and guided her aside so that the two men with the large valise could pass. He noted that they were met by two others, also well-armed; and he heard the soft exchange of greetings.

"No trouble?"

"None. The General must be slipping. Just the same, I'll be glad to see it in the company safe."

"Walk on ahead. We'll cover you from a ways back."

This was none of his business, and Cohoon turned to the girl, using her in that moment as a kind of anchor to reality. Concentrating on being polite and helpful to her, he could delay briefly the full impact of the changes he was going to have to face. He did not want to look around to see if there was anyone in the crowd he recognized. Someone who had kept count of the days could have worked out the probable time of his arrival here; but he had sent no message ahead, and no one came forward to greet him now.

"I'll help you with your things," he said, reaching for the small bag as the driver handed it down. But the girl stepped forward and reached it first.

"Thank you just the same," she said. "If you'd just see that my trunk gets off—it's the little brown one up there—I'll send for it later. And if you'd tell me where I can find Miss Elizabeth Tomkins. The place is on Creek Lane, wherever that may be."

There was a brief silence that involved not only Cohoon

8

and the driver but several other men and a pair of women standing nearby, all of whom looked sharply at the girl before resuming their talk. The driver spat and turned away. Cohoon regarded the girl for a moment. She was fairly tall and nicely shaped, he saw, with brown hair, gray eyes, a straight nose, and a long, humorous mouth. She was conservatively dressed in a dark green traveling suit that had a fashionable look despite the ravages of the long, dusty journey.

This was none of his business either, but the attitudes of the bystanders annoyed him; people were very quick to hurt and reject, as he had learned from experience. He reached for the bag she was holding and took it from her.

"I'll show you the way, ma'am," he said.

"It's not necessary. You've been very kind." There was a look of wry amusement, not entirely lacking in bitterness, in the girl's eyes, and he understood that she was fully aware of the situation.

"Come on," he said impatiently, setting off across the street at a good pace, so that it took her a few seconds to catch up. They passed the familiar weathered front of Van Houck's trading post, that had at one time been the only building within a hundred miles—but that had been even before Cohoon's time. He turned right at the corner.

"Creek Lane," he said, with a glance at his companion. "Miss Bessie's place is the one with the two-headed bird on it; I presume she's still doing business at the same address. The Double Eagle. Don't let the tame look of the street deceive you. It's early yet."

He stopped in front of the building, and held out the small valise, which she took. "Thank you," she said.

"My pleasure."

"It wasn't wise of you to help me," she said. "If you live here. They'll tear you apart for it. Charity is a word that sounds fine in church on Sunday, but this isn't Sunday."

He grinned. "Ma'am, after five years in Yuma, I figure it's a little late to start worrying about what people are going to say."

She had turned toward the door. Now she swung back, startled, and looked at him in silence for a moment. "Yuma? That's the Territorial Prison, isn't it?"

"Yes, ma'am."

"What did you do, hold up a stagecoach?"

"Yes, ma'am."

She was a little taken aback by his ready assent. "Well, I wouldn't have guessed it to look at you," she said.

9

Cohoon drawled, with a glance at the saloon door, "I wouldn't have guessed it to look at you, either, ma'am."

The girl laughed, but when she spoke again there was a defensive hardness in her voice. "Well, some evening when you're not holding up stages, you can come around and hear me sing and have a drink on the house for your kindness. If you don't see me, ask for Nan Montoya. Mrs. Nan Montoya." She laughed again, and the hardness of the sound was tinged with bitterness. "Montoya is dead, if it matters; and I was never legally married to him, anyway."

2

THE SUN WAS OFF the street as he walked back the way he had come, but the baked dusty earth and the walls of the buildings he passed still radiated the heat of the day. At the corner of Main Street, he turned right. In this direction, the town soon ended in a scattering of shacks and adobe huts, beyond which the church stood on a small rise where the sun still shone, but this light faded before he reached the white gate. He stepped inside and made his way among the headstones on the hillside to a group of four graves.

There had been only two the last time he had been here: that of his oldest brother, Stuart, who had been killed by a raiding party of Apaches when Cohoon was fourteen; and that of his mother, who had died two years later. Now there were two more, and he read the inscriptions: *Jonathan Walker Cohoon, 1859-1885,* and *Ward Zachariah Cohoon, 1816-1885.* It occurred to him, as a small surprise, that he had not until this moment known the date of his father's birth.

He removed his hat and knelt awkwardly, feeling hypocritical in the act since he had not had much practice—particularly of late—in the niceties of religious observance. Yet some token of respect and love was necessary. He had never been close to his father, but he had admired and revered him, and envied the two older brothers who, in size, endurance, courage, and ability, had more closely lived up to the standards Ward Cohoon had set for his sons.

Kneeling there, he felt as inadequate in the presence of the silent stone marker as he had always felt in the physical presence of the great, shaggy, buckskin-clad figure of the man who had been his father. He remembered clearly the fascinated horror with which, as a child, he had regarded the scalps that Ward Cohoon had carried at his belt until his wife finally persuaded him to lay them aside; he recalled his own frustration, and his father's impatience—and the open scorn of his brothers—as he tried time and again to master to his father's satisfaction whatever weapon had been selected for the day's practice. He had been his mother's best pupil, and his father's worst; and the ease with which Stuart and Jonathan picked up the knack of rifle, knife, and tomahawk—although they never did learn to read and write properly—had deepened Boyd Cohoon's awareness of his own inadequacy.

Well, he reflected now, there was no sense in pretending to be something you weren't, and people were just going to have to get along with one Cohoon who stood and acted something less than seven feet tall. He rose and brushed off his knees, put his hat back on and stood for a moment looking at the four graves. *Well, you're on your own now, my friend,* he told himself, and turned and walked back into town.

In front of Van Houck's store he paused; after a moment he went inside. The old bearded trader was at the back of the store, counting his receipts of the day in preparation for closing up. Without looking up, he shook his head imperatively at Cohoon's approach, to indicate that he would lose count if he were interrupted. Cohoon leaned against the counter, waiting. Presently the old man closed the money box, raised his head, and peered at his visitor through steel-rimmed glasses.

"Five years is a long time, Uncle Van," Cohoon said. "How's my credit? I need an outfit."

Van Houck frowned briefly; then his eyes widened with recognition, and he came quickly around the counter to grasp Cohoon by the shoulders, almost shaking him.

"My boy! I did not realize—" He pulled Cohoon toward the front of the store where the light was better. "Help yourself to anything you need, but first let me look at you. Ah, but it is a man now! Almost as big as your father. . . ." His smile faded abruptly, and he looked up at the younger man. "Did you get my letter, in that place?"

"Yes," Cohoon said. After a moment, he said, "You didn't write *how* it happened, Uncle Van."

The old trader said, "It was like a stroke of lightning. I have grown soft, my boy. In the old days, one heard of friends and their families wiped out by the Apaches, and one said a prayer for their souls and checked the loading of the guns and the shutters for the windows. But these are less violent times, and to hear of your father dead, shot in the back within five miles

11

of town, after all the places he had been. . . . It was like waking up one morning to find that the great rock out there had fallen from its pedestal. And when the men came back with the news that Jonathan and the cook had also been shot down, out at the ranch, and the house burned . . . !"

Cohoon asked, "Was it the Apaches, Uncle Van?"

Van Houck shook his head. "There are some who would like us to think so, but it was no Apache. One man it was, with iron shoes on his horse. I am too old to ride with posses, but I heard the men talk when they came back—those that were not afraid to talk, or in Westerman's pay. One horse. One man. He met your father outside of town. Whether the meeting had been arranged or was an accident no one knows. They talked for a while. Your father turned to ride away. Would he have turned his back on an Apache, after fifty years on the plains? The man shot him. The stock of your father's rifle was broken off short; he had tried to pull the gun out as he fell, and snapped it off at the grip instead. The broken wood was still in his hands when he was found."

Cohoon said, "And Jonathan?"

"The murderer rode directly to the ranch. Perhaps he was afraid that Jonathan knew whom your father had gone out to meet; perhaps he just realized that he would have to deal with Jonathan sooner or later, and preferred to take him unawares. Jonathan was shot as he opened the door. Would Jonathan have opened the door to an Apache, without even a gun in his hand? The murderer then shot down the cook, old Leonardo, as he ran for the corral, and set fire to the house. When the hands got there—they were working to the east— two hours or more had passed. They lost the trail up in the rocks. The posse caught up with them while they were still trying to work it out. Finally Westerman said to call it a day; it was obviously the work of a prowling Indian, and he would notify the authorities."

"Paul Westerman led the posse?" Cohoon said.

"Yes. We still have no law here, my boy, except when the U.S. Marshal condescends to pay us a visit. Well, now we've got a town marshal of sorts to keep order here in Sombrero, but he was out of town and this was out of his jurisdiction anyway. Westerman rounded up a group of citizens and made a little speech, saying that at a time like this personal feelings were unimportant; a crime like this was a threat to every member of the community, and the criminal had to be caught and punished."

"That was public-spirited of Mr. Westerman," Cohoon drawled.

Van Houck was watching him. "Boyd, what are you going to do?"

Cohoon hesitated, and moved his shoulders slightly. "What can I do, Uncle Van? The man apparently left no clues except a set of hoof-prints leading nowhere. What can I do against a ghost?"

"This was no ghost," Van Houck said harshly, "and no Apache, either. We know who it was, Boyd. It was a white man; a white man with a burning hate against the Cohoons. The same man who tried so hard to put a rope around your neck at the trial; who publicly proclaimed, when you were led away to prison, that the matter was not finished yet."

Cohoon said mildly, "You can't put too much weight on what a grief-stricken man says and does, Uncle Van. Harry's death hit him hard, and he blamed me for it. He is the type of man who must blame somebody for everything that happens to him."

Van Houck said, "Ah, that Harry Westerman was a no-good young trouble-maker, and you should have had more brains than to get mixed up with him. I must say that I still do not believe everything that was said at the trial, nor do a great many other people, Boyd." The old man looked searchingly into the face of his visitor, who laughed shortly.

"I'm glad for everybody's good opinion, but it's a matter of public record, and I've never denied it. But there's one thing wrong with your choice of a murderer, Uncle Van."

"What's that?"

"Why," Cohoon said, "neither Father nor Jonathan were fools. The fact that neither was holding a gun when he died may prove it was no Apache that killed them, but it also proves to my satisfaction that it wasn't Paul Westerman. They wouldn't have trusted him any farther than an Indian."

Van Houck shrugged, totally unconvinced. "So? Then he hired somebody. He hires many people these days. A stranger perhaps?"

Cohoon said, "Perhaps. But there's no proof of that."

The old trader stared at him. "You are going to do nothing, Boyd? You are just going to forget it?"

"It would be a little hard to forget, Uncle Van," Cohoon said gently. "However, I have just spent five years of my life waiting to get out of prison; I don't intend to turn around and shoot my way right back in again—on no more than a shaky guess."

"Your father—"

"I know," Cohoon said. "Father would have gone roaring after Westerman and challenged him to prove his innocence. So would Jonathan, or Stuart, if they had lived. But I'm not any of them. That's one thing I discovered in Yuma." He looked down at Van Houck and smiled. "You know, Uncle Van, I learned something in that place. I never was as big as the rest of them, or as handy with weapons, and I couldn't hold as much liquor or make as much noise, but in Yuma I was a better man than any of them. They would have tried to buck the system, and it would have broken and killed them. I rode along with it, and here I am. Now you want me to buck this system and get myself killed or hanged. Well, if you don't mind, Uncle Van, I reckon I'll just ride along with it for a piece, like I did in Yuma."

Van Houck said harshly, "Maybe this will make you change your mind." He turned and marched to the rear of the store, his back stiff and angry. Returning, he threw down three objects on the nearby counter. "I saved these for you. I thought you would be needing them. The gun can be repaired. I have also, by your father's will, paid the taxes on the Grant from the money he had in the bank; there's enough left to help you get started again. Of course you need no money for anything I can supply."

Cohoon looked for a moment at the broken Henry rifle, and the splintered stock that lay beside it, touching the latter gently. "Thanks, Uncle Van."

Van Houck's voice said, "He had it in his hands when he was found. He never got to use it!"

Cohoon turned to the knife in its worn leather sheath and pulled it free. The blade was hand-ground of file steel. The leather grip, as well as the sheath, had been burned with the Cohoons' Diamond C brand. Cohoon spoke softly:

"He always said that a good knife was worth a dozen pistols in a fight; and when there was nobody to fight you could always whittle."

"You're going to let his murderer go free?" Van Houck asked insistently. "You're going to live in the same town with the man who killed him, and do nothing?"

Cohoon set the knife back into the sheath with a sharp movement. "Why, I can stand it as long as he can, Uncle Van," he murmured. "Maybe even a little longer. It remains to be seen."

14

3

OUTSIDE THE AIR was quite cool, and Cohoon drew a deep breath of it, turned left, and walked quickly away. The heavy-set, bearded man who chose this moment to come out of the alley between the buildings was also moving in a hurried manner. There was time for neither man to stop. The impact threw Cohoon sideways, and sent the other back a step with a hand to his shoulder, gouged by the barrel of the broken rifle in Cohoon's hand. The man was dressed, Cohoon noted, in the rough stained clothing of a prospector or miner.

"My apologies," Cohoon said mildly, although the fault had been by no means entirely his.

"Apologies! Why the hell don't you watch where you're going?"

There was no profit in this, and Cohoon turned and walked on. He had taken three steps when the other's hand swung him about so roughly that the weapons he was carrying spun out of his grasp.

"I asked you a question, stranger. Why the hell don't you watch where the hell you're going?"

Cohoon looked at the bearded face for a moment, not really hearing the words, feeling only the contemptuous hand on his shoulder that reminded him of the brutalities and indignities he had suffered without protest for five years, knowing that was the only way to survive. But this was not Yuma. This man had no badge, and the law was not behind him.

Cohoon spoke softly. "Take your hand away."

"Why, you young pipsqueak—"

Cohoon drew a long breath. The bearded face seemed to swim before him in a kind of shimmering haze, but his mind was quite clear despite the anger. His muscles tightened imperceptibly in preparation for the quick seizing of the hairy wrist, the pivot, and the throw that would send the other over his shoulder into the dust of the street below, followed by his own body, feet-first, driving hard to crack the ribs and empty the lungs, after which the boots could finish the job at leisure. There had been no gentlemanly eastern rules taught in those daily practice sessions out by the corral. *Never give the other man a break until he's out cold,* had been Ward Cohoon's repeated advice to his sons.

Cohoon turned slightly, casually, for better leverage, and instinct made him cast a glance around to fix in his mind the location of others who might intervene—and slowly he let his pent-up breath escape, because the street was quite still, waiting, and over by the hotel stood a slender man in dark clothes on whose shirt-front glinted the metallic emblem of the law. He should have recognized that waiting silence the instant he came out of the store, but he had been in too much of a hurry to escape Van Houck's reproachful gaze. This was a trap. This was Paul Westerman's marshal, ready to throw an ex-convict in jail on any excuse. A brawl would be reason enough for the law to take a hand.

Cohoon reached up and gently disengaged the hand from his shoulder and let it fall. "I'm sorry, partner," he said. "Reckon I was a little careless. No harm intended."

The bearded man was confused by the sudden lack of opposition. He growled without conviction, "No harm? Why, you like to broke my shoulder! Somebody ought to teach you to look out where you wave that gun barrel!"

Cohoon said, "I'm sorry. I'll be more careful in the future."

The larger man stared at him in a baffled way, and looked around, as if for a cue or signal. Then he said, "Ah, hell," and swung away, and strode off down the boardwalk.

Cohoon watched him go, aware that around him the scene was breaking into motion again as people started off about their business, some looking at him curiously, others ignoring him. It seemed strange that he should recognize none of them; five years before, an unfamiliar face would have been an exception on the streets of Sombrero. He grimaced, picked up his belongings, and started toward the hotel.

"Cohoon."

It was the slender man with the badge, who had crossed over and come up this side of the street. Cohoon waited for him, watching him approach. At close range, it was apparent that the marshal was much younger than he had seemed at a distance. The neat, somber clothes, that might have belonged to a preacher, except for the badge of office and the heavy gun and belt, were deceiving. The face was that of a man a year or two younger than Cohoon himself. It was a sober and humorless face despite its youth, clean-shaven, and set in stern lines—it was the face of a young man constantly aware that the eyes of his fellow citizens were upon him.

Recognition struck Cohoon quite suddenly, and he spoke without thinking, "My God. It's Willie Black!"

He saw the young marshal wince slightly, and realized his mistake. He had been undiplomatic, remembering the thin, dirty kid who, cursed and kicked by his drunken parent, used to hold the horses and tend the lines at Black's Ferry. He remembered also the hatred on Willie Black's pale face when they had pulled him out of the river that day after Jonathan's practical joke—Jonathan's humor, like his father's, had been heavy-handed at times. But it would be Bill Black now, marshal of Sombrero, and no thanks to anyone who reminded him of the past.

"What are your plans, Cohoon?" Black asked, stopping before him.

Cohoon moved his shoulders briefly and did not speak.

"I'm giving you fair warning," the marshal said. "The time is past when the Cohoons could ride into this town and take it apart for their own amusement. When you visit Sombrero from now on, do so peaceably, or by God I'll arrest you and send you right back to the place from which you've just come. I don't care if your folks came into this country with Coronado. To me you're just another tough one who got himself caught."

It was a harsh speech, deliberately provoking; and Cohoon looked at the younger man with wonder and some amusement. "That's the second fight I've had offered me in two minutes," he murmured.

Black flushed, and the old hatred showed clearly in his eyes. He said stiffly, "I am merely doing my duty, which is to keep the peace."

"I'm not the one who's threatening it," Cohoon said, and walked on.

The lamps were already lighted in the hotel when he entered. The clerk at the desk addressed him by name and had a room key ready for him. Cohoon looked at the key and pursed his lips.

"Room twenty-one," the clerk said, a little too quickly.

Cohoon nodded, picked up the small grip that had been put off the stage for him, and climbed the stairs. The room was on the right hand side of the dank and narrow hall, halfway down. Light showed under the ill-fitting door. Cohoon whistled a soundless tune, and shifted the objects he was carrying in such a way that his father's heavy knife was ready to his hand. He unlocked the door with the key, and let it swing open.

The man sitting on the bed said, "Welcome home, Boyd."

17

Cohoon nodded, stepped inside, kicked the door shut, and dropped his belongings onto a nearby chair, except for the broken rifle, which he leaned against the dresser.

"There was your bully-boy," he said, "and your tame marshal, and now there's you, Mr. Westerman."

"You do young Black an injustice," Paul Westerman said. "He's his own man. I merely use him, without his knowledge."

"Which brings up the question," Cohoon said, "is it worse to be crooked, or stupid?"

Westerman smiled. "There's whisky on the dresser, Boyd. Help yourself. Sit down. We have a number of things to talk about. . . . Thanks, I'll have one too. Good whisky is its own excuse, in any company."

Cohoon picked up a straight-backed wooden chair and swung it about so that he could straddle it. Sitting down, he glanced around the room and saw no hiding place for another man, although there were doubtless others, well-armed, in the adjoining room that was separated from this one only by a flimsy door. Even five years ago, Paul Westerman had seldom gone anywhere unescorted. Not so much that he needed protection, as that he obviously liked the feeling of power it gave him to have armed men at his back. This was necessary to him, since he was a small man.

Five years had been kind to him, Cohoon saw. The added stockiness time had brought to his short figure only gave it dignity, and this was emphasized by the gray that had appeared at his temples: for all his lack of height, Paul Westerman made an impressive appearance nowadays. His clothes were conservative and well cut—even five years ago he had still clung to some habits of dress from his gambling days, but these were gone now. It was hard to remember, looking at him, that this man had once worked in one of the shabbier places on Creek Lane, when Creek Lane was little more than a cluster of ill-favored shanties. He probably owned the Lane by now; he had been well on the way five years ago. Perhaps, Cohoon reflected, he owned this hotel as well; at least it was obvious that he owned the clerk at the desk.

"I brought no gun, if that's what you're looking for," Westerman said abruptly.

Cohoon thought this was unlikely; an ex-gambler would have a derringer or similar weapon concealed somewhere, no matter how respectable his outward appearance had become. But there was nothing to be gained by arguing the point.

"Neither did I," Cohoon said, "except for that." He indicated the broken rifle with a jerk of his head.

18

Westerman smiled. "In your father's hands, the knife on that chair was the equal of any revolver. I'd be surprised if he hadn't taught you how to use it." Cohoon did not speak. Westerman's smile faded, and was replaced by a look of grave sympathy. "I was genuinely sorry to hear of his death, Boyd, and that of your brother, and I did my best to help catch the murderer. I want you to believe that. I also want you to believe that I had no part in the crime, as has undoubtedly been suggested to you already. I like to think that I have a logical mind. I want to see justice done—some might call it vengeance —but I would not want anybody to think I had ventured upon an irrational blood feud. I had nothing against the rest of your family, and I had nothing to do with those killings, Boyd. I want you to believe me, really I do."

"Does it matter?" Cohoon asked.

Westerman spread his hands and shrugged. "Perhaps not. Your opinion isn't very important, is it? You were a fool to come back. If you had just vanished into thin air after your release—well, as I say, I have a logical mind, and an economical one. Why should I bother to spend time and money chasing after you? It would not bring Harry back, and a hatred can starve in five years with nothing to feed it. I would have let you go. But instead you came back here to remind me. . . . That boy was everything to me, Boyd. My one sentimentality. He reminded me of his mother who gave her life to bear him. He wasn't much good, Boyd, I am aware of that. I don't deceive myself that my boy was an angel. Nevertheless, he was mine, and you took him from me."

"Hardly that, Mr. Westerman," Cohoon said mildly. "It was one of the passengers who shot Harry, not I."

A spasm of anger crossed Westerman's face. "And you were supposed to cover the passengers; that was your job! If you had to involve my boy in a robbery, you could at least have done your share! Instead of which you took to your heels like a rabbit at the first sign of trouble and left Harry to be shot down by that fool of a drummer with his bulldog revolver!"

"After Harry had first shot the guard in cold blood," Cohoon said dryly. "Perhaps I hadn't bargained for deliberate murder, Mr. Westerman."

"Oh, I'm sure you had the highest motives for deserting your partner!" Westerman said sarcastically. "No Cohoon could simply lose his nerve and run, could he? Nevertheless, Harry is dead. I took care of that drummer years ago—something I regret now, since the man could hardly be blamed for taking advantage of his opportunity. But you, who gave him the opportunity . . . !" Westerman checked himself abruptly and rose. "That was five years ago, Boyd. I am not a monomaniac. As I say, I regret having had that poor man killed, but it was done in the heat of passion. There's no passion left in me now. I simply can't stand having you around." He picked up his hat and walked to the door. "If you leave Sombrero by the first stage out, no one will follow you. You can pick up your life somewhere else, and you will not be harmed as long as you never come back here. If you choose to stay, however, I will not answer for the consequences. That's what I came here to say, Boyd. Good day."

4

IT WAS QUITE dark when Cohoon, having shaved and washed in his room, came out of the hotel. As he walked along Main Street, the food odors emanating from the Pioneer Café reminded him that he had not eaten for the better part of a day, but he did not stop until he reached the new bank building. There he paused to check on something that had caught his eye as he rode by on the stage. The gold-leaf lettering on the door was clean and bright: THE MINERS AND STOCK-MENS BANK—*Roger St. Cloud Paradine, Pres.*

Cohoon nodded thoughtfully, turned, and walked back a block the way he had come, swinging into the side street to the south. He was aware of the night noises about him: the sound of adult voices raised for one reason or another here and there throughout the town, the shrill cries of children, the barking of dogs, the beat of hoofs and the rattle of wheels— after five years, all these sounds were new and rich in meaning. Out on the desert, a coyote threw his yapping howl at the night sky; on Creek Lane somebody fired a gun three times. Cohoon was reminded of the assured, embittered young woman he had delivered to Miss Bessie's place, but she was still none of his business.

When he reached it, the Paradine house looked smaller than he remembered it. Once it had stood alone here, and people had laughed at Colonel Paradine's notion of building his town house in a back alley—and one that was under running water a couple of times a year, at that. Now it seemed that, protected by rude rock levees, Arroyo Street had become the choice residential thoroughfare of the town; and the Paradine house was only one of a dozen or more fairly pretentious frame dwellings, very different from the predominantly adobe architecture of the rest of the community.

There were lights in the house. Cohoon walked up to the door, hearing his boots strike hollowly on the porch. It seemed ridiculous that he should be more afraid tonight than the first night he had come here as a boy of seventeen. He knocked, and waited, hearing footsteps approach through the house.

Francis Paradine opened the door. Cohoon was surprised to see him; somehow young Paradine had practically slipped his memory, which was odd under the circumstances. Francis had been a thin, girlish, blond boy with a dissatisfied mouth; five years had turned him into a sleek, plump blond young man. The change was startling, but could hardly be called an improvement.

As he stepped inside, Cohoon heard Mrs. Paradine's voice call from upstairs: "Francis, Francis, who is it, darling?"

"It's all right, Mother," Francis called back. "It's just somebody for Claire."

He closed the door, and looked at Cohoon. Their eyes were about on a level. There was no expression at all in Francis Paradine's face. His look was as blandly polite and meaningless as if the man facing him had been a complete stranger.

"She's in there," he said, jerking his head toward the room which, Cohoon recalled, was known as the study or library. "She's waiting for you. Excuse me, I'd better go to Mother. She's not feeling well tonight."

Cohoon watched him mount the stairs, noting that Francis moved with a slight limp. He grimaced at a memory. Mrs. Paradine, upstairs, raised her voice fretfully; and it seemed that nothing had changed much after all. Cohoon could recall a time when Mrs. Paradine's health had been a matter of great importance to him. He had never entered the house without inquiring about it, or left without expressing hope that it would be improved tomorrow. Now, somehow, he knew that it would never improve; it was a weapon that Mrs. Paradine used against her husband and family, for some reason that was not clear. You could figure out a number of things like that in five years.

A movement caused him to look quickly toward the library door, which had opened. Claire Paradine stood there.

"If you won't come to me, Boyd," she said quietly, "I suppose I'll have to come to you."

21

He had lived this moment a thousand times in imagination; he would have said that he had anticipated every form it could possibly take. He had imagined her greeting him with open arms outside the prison gate; there had also been times when he had visualized her having him turned away from the door. The one possibility which he had not conceived was that, at this moment, they would simply stand and look at each other across the hall.

Presently he moved forward, not knowing clearly what was in his own mind, and having no idea what was in hers. Perhaps he was hoping that she would come to meet him or give him some sign, at least, of feeling for him; some excuse for taking her into his arms. But she had never been a demonstrative girl; she had always been afraid of emotion, he remembered, in herself as well as in others. She stepped back now, letting him pass without touching her; when he was inside the library, she closed the door behind him and leaned against it.

He spoke casually, "I see your dad's a banker now, Claire."

"Why, yes," she said quickly, grateful to him for introducing the subject. "He gave up the ranch about a year after . . . about four years ago. Didn't I write you?"

"No," he said, "you didn't write me, Claire."

She went on, a little breathlessly, "Well, it was mostly for Mother's sake; she couldn't stand the heat and dust out at the ranch. Besides, Dad never was much of a cattleman, anyway."

Her voice was tinged with a kind of affectionate contempt. Reared in a very different family atmosphere, Cohoon had never quite become accustomed to the attitude the younger Paradines displayed toward their male parent. Apparently this, too, remained the way it had been. But everything was not the same, as he saw when at last he turned to look at her directly. *Why*, he thought, *why, we were children!*

They were children no longer. Reading his thoughts, Claire Paradine flushed slightly. Her voice went on, however, hurriedly.

"Well, everybody started finding silver in the San Pedros and Catalans, and the town began to grow like a mushroom, and there wasn't a bank for all the money between here and Tucson. . . . Well, you know how Dad likes to think himself a financial wizard. He sold the ranch to a man named DeValla, and we moved to town for good. . . ." Her voice died away. At last she whispered, "Well, Boyd?"

They were both silent then. After a moment Claire pushed

herself away from the door, standing straight and slim, facing him deliberately, as if ashamed of the weakness that had caused her to seek support. She was wearing a pale blue dress; she had always been partial to blue, he recalled. Her fair hair was put up in a neat and ladylike manner; he remembered when she had worn it otherwise. She was a small girl but not diminutive by any means; she looked thoroughly feminine without giving any impression of helplessness or fragility. He remembered that she had once scrambled down to the river with him, below Black's Ferry where the canyon was reputed to be impregnable. Looking at her now as she stood there, adult and lovely, the memory seemed a little incredible.

He remembered that; and he remembered another day when he had come to town in the wagon and they had driven to the river again by a way they had discovered through the hills—a reckless act, since a ranch to the south had been burned by hostiles only a week earlier. But the river had a special meaning for them in those days, and at seventeen and nineteen, in love, you're practically immortal. They had wandered too far along the canyon, following the north rim; then, trying to discover a short way back to town with the team and wagon, they had lost themselves and found it necessary to follow their own tracks out. Darkness had found them still in the hills. He had been worrying, he remembered, mainly about the reception he would meet upon bringing Claire home so late. The Paradines did not really approve of him.

He had been driving the team hard along the rudimentary trail, making enough noise for a stage and four. If it had not been for the moonlight, they would have passed the horse and rider in the dark without ever knowing it. As it was, Cohoon caught a glimpse of motion in the hills to the right, snatched up the rifle lying behind him in the wagon, and tossed the reins to Claire, shouting to her over the clattering noise of the wheels not to stop for anything; he'd get in back and try to hold them off.

Vague thoughts of heroic death had passed through his mind, he remembered; the kind of thoughts you had at nineteen. As he recalled, the plan uppermost in his mind had involved dropping off the wagon at a suitable spot and making a gallant, last-ditch stand, holding the savages at bay long enough for Claire to reach safety. It was something of an anticlimax, therefore, when he saw, as they topped the next rise, the horse still standing where he had last seen it with the rider no longer in the saddle. Claire, too, had been looking

23

back; he remembered the way she had sawed the team to a stop.

"Why," she had gasped in the sudden silence, "why, that's Frankie's horse!"

The boy had been unconscious when they reached him, half dead from loss of blood. A bullet had smashed his thigh. The black silk still about his neck, with the eyeholes in it, told most of the story—although it was only later that they learned of Harry Westerman's part in the business. After checking the bleeding as best they could, Claire and Cohoon had looked at each other in the bright moonlight. There was already a sound of many horsemen to the east. Cohoon had untied the mask from about Francis's neck and stuffed it into his own pocket.

"Take him to our place," he had said. "You'll have to cut west and cross at Yellow Ford; they'll have sent a man or two to watch the Ferry, coming that way. Father knows all about bullet wounds; he'll take care of it until you can get a doctor out. Dr. Bell will keep his mouth shut, I reckon, if your dad talks to him."

She had not asked what he was planning to do; his intentions had been clear enough. He could remember that she had hesitated, and looked down at her unconscious brother. Then she had drawn a long breath, turned to Cohoon, and kissed him; after all, they were in love, and it was inconceivable that anything could happen to either of them. He had lifted Francis into the wagon with her help; then he had climbed onto the boy's lathered horse and ridden away. After all, it was only a little thing he was about to do now; a moment before he had been prepared to die for her.

The posse caught him after the horse gave out; the Paradines had a fondness for fast and pretty horses, and this had been a place for neither speed nor looks, only endurance, which the beast had not possessed. He had destroyed it at the edge of the river, letting its final struggles carry it over the canyon edge at a spot where, even if it were discovered, no one would be likely to climb down to look for clues as to its owner's identity.

Even then, knowing the country well, he could probably have evaded them had he shot the Papago tracker leading them. Twice he had the man in his sights; but it was, of course, out of the question for him to kill anybody, even an Indian. In jail, he had refused to speak for the first day; then she had come, but not alone. Colonel Paradine had been with her.

The Colonel had sent the guard out of earshot, and made his speech. His son's condition was critical; it would kill the

24

boy to be moved, or even disturbed. It would kill Mrs. Paradine to learn that her son had been involved. . . . Cohoon had not listened to the words. He had watched Claire's face; and he had known what she would say by the fact that she would not meet his eyes.

"I'll wait," she had whispered. "I'll wait for you."

There had been, of course, no choice. At nineteen. Once you started being a hero you could not back out even if you wanted to.

5

THAT HAD BEEN five years ago. Now he started to speak, and checked himself, not clear in his mind as to what he wanted to say. She made a small gesture, without meaning; he took a step forward, and she turned up her face for the kiss. Her lips were cool and remote; her hands pressed lightly against his chest, maintaining a safe distance between them. Cohoon released her and stepped back.

Claire was the first to speak. "I waited," she whispered. "I kept my promise, Boyd. I . . . I can't help it if . . . if . . ." There were tears in her eyes. "I'm sorry," she breathed. "I'm sorry."

"Yes," he said, and the drawl that he often used to mask his feelings was in his voice. "Well, I reckon I'll be going. Give my regards to your folks."

He turned to the door. Claire made a protesting sound, but whatever she had been about to say was lost in a noise from the hall. They heard Francis's voice:

"Mother, please!"

Then the door swung open, and Mrs. Paradine was standing there. "Well, really!" she said. "I declare, I wouldn't have believed it if Francis hadn't told me! Young man, I'm amazed that you dare set foot in the home of decent and law-abiding people; but then, I suppose one can't expect consideration from a—"

"Mother!" said Claire sharply; and Colonel Paradine was there, taking his wife by the arm. "Don't excite yourself, Elinor," the Colonel said smoothly. "I'll take care of this. Francis, help your mother back to her room."

Mrs. Paradine did not move immediately. Cohoon studied the thin figure in the doorway, seeing a distorted and uncomfortable reflection of the daughter in the petulant mouth and sharply pretty features of the older woman. He bowed slightly.

"I'm sorry to have upset you, ma'am," he said. "I was just taking my leave."

Mrs. Paradine's anger seemed to fade abruptly before his courtesy. "Well," she said, "well, I'm real sorry if I seem harsh, Boyd, but one has to maintain a few standards, even in this forsaken country."

"I understand," Cohoon said. "I should not have intruded. It's only natural that you would not want a jailbird in your home."

He made his way past her, and walked quickly down the hall toward the front door. Pausing to retrieve the hat he had laid aside there, he heard the whisper of skirts behind him and turned to face Claire. Her face was quite pale.

"Boyd!" she whispered, keeping her voice low. "Oh, Boyd, what can I say? She doesn't know; she doesn't understand. You mustn't think—"

The thing had gone beyond anger or bitterness; there was nothing left to do but laugh, which he did. "Take it easy, Claire," he said. "The mistake was mine. Five years is a long time. Too long, I reckon."

"Please, Boyd! I don't want you to hate us, although you have every right."

The Colonel came quickly down the hall to join them, putting a hand on Cohoon's arm. "I'm sorry for the misunderstanding, Boyd. Please accept my apology." The older man cleared his throat, and looked around to make certain his wife was out of hearing. "If you'd come back into the library, I'd like to talk to you, my boy."

They all shared certain features, these Paradines, Cohoon found himself thinking; they were all blond, with the pale skin and eyes of overbreeding. The Colonel was a straight, small-ish man with thinning hair, a long face, and a neat yellow mustache which he liked to caress with a forefinger, doing it now as he waited for Cohoon's response.

"Please, Boyd," Claire said, reaching for his hat. He allowed her to take it and lay it aside again. He walked between the two of them back the way he had come. In the library, Colonel Paradine closed the door and turned the key in the lock.

"Mrs. Paradine does not, of course, know the true situation, or she would not have spoken as she did," he said, coming forward. "She must never know. Her health is very poor these days, Boyd. The shock might well be too much for her. . . . Sit down, my boy. Over here by the desk. Claire, perhaps it would be better if you let us talk in private."

The girl shook her head and seated herself on the sofa, composing herself in a graceful and ladylike manner. She was an attractive stranger, no one he had ever known, and Cohoon could hardly believe that he had kissed her, even if it had not been much of a kiss.

"Very well." Colonel Paradine apparently knew better than to argue with his daughter. He walked around the desk and sat down. "Now, then, let's discuss the situation sensibly. The fact of the matter, Boyd, is very simply this: at considerable cost to yourself you have saved this family untold shame and anguish. We owe you a tremendous debt. Please don't think for a moment that we're not aware of it." He cleared his throat impressively. "We can, of course, never make up to you a fraction of what you must have suffered in that place. It would be presumptuous of us to try. I—er—gather that there was at one time some kind of a romantic understanding between you and my daughter. That, of course, is for the two of you to settle between you."

"It's settled," Cohoon said dryly.

The Colonel glanced quickly toward his daughter; what he saw on her face seemed to give him satisfaction. "I see," he said crisply. "Well, in that case, there is nothing left but for me to do what little I can to make things up to you. As I say, I wouldn't even try to compensate you for the mental and physical anguish you must have endured. Fortunately, however, I am in a position to offer you some slight recompense for the five years of your life you have sacrificed for us. I am fully aware that this will not begin to wipe out the debt we owe you; so if there's anything further I can ever do for you, Boyd, I expect you to get in touch with me." He opened a drawer of his desk and brought out a paper-wrapped package. "Five years," he said, "at a nominal salary of two thousand dollars a year would come to ten thousand dollars, which you'll find here. It's a poor repayment for what you've been through, but it will at least help you make a new start somewhere. As I say, if there's ever anything else I can do, don't hesitate to let me know."

Cohoon looked at the package on the desk, and at the long, mustached face of the man behind the desk. Well, he thought, you had to hand it to the Paradines; they never did things by halves. When they let you down, they let you down all the way. And when they slapped your face with money, they didn't spare the greenbacks. Ten thousand dollars, clear profit, wasn't bad

27

for five years' work. Men had spent their lives out here, and died, without ever seeing a fraction of that sum.

He turned his head slowly to look at the girl on the sofa; for some reason it was important for him to know if she had been aware this was coming. The answer was plain on her face; she looked pleased by the magnanimity of her father's gesture, perhaps feeling that it atoned for the poverty of her own greeting. Cohoon drew a long breath and rose. It was the time for a courteous refusal and a quick withdrawal; but suddenly he found himself hating these people. It was unbearable to think that they should get five years of his life for nothing. He had to exact some payment, even if only in bank notes that he could never bring himself to use.

He reached for the package. "Thank you, sir," he said deliberately, dropping it into his pocket. "That's more than generous."

"Our gratitude goes with it, Boyd," the Colonel said smoothly. "Good luck. And when you decide on a place to settle down, write us. We don't like to lose track of our friends."

Outside, the air was cool as Cohoon walked swiftly away, holding himself under control with an effort. There was no sense in a man's going around kicking stray dogs or bruising his fist against adobe walls just because people had acted in a manner anyone but a romantic boy should have been able to predict. . . . Only gradually, as he relived the scene in his mind, did the strangeness of the Colonel's final words reach his consciousness. Colonel Paradine seemed to take for granted that he, Boyd Cohoon, was leaving this part of the country; this assumption had colored other parts of his speech as well. Yet Paul Westerman had delivered his ultimatum privately less than an hour ago, hardly time for the news to have reached Arroyo Street by the path of rumor. It seemed almost as if the Paradines must have known of Westerman's intention in advance. . . .

Cohoon glanced back at the big, lighted house, frowning; then a movement in the shadows brought him around quickly, his hand sliding back to the knife that was his only weapon, since his disagreement with Van Houck had caused him to forget the necessity for buying a revolver. Besides, his father had always considered the knife adequate as long as the odds were reasonable, carrying two old revolving pistols in saddle holsters for use against Indians, but seldom bothering to wear one on his person.

"Oh, it's you, Willie," Cohoon said, straightening up, as

28

Marshal Black stepped into the light. "What are you doing in this part of town? I'd think Creek Lane would need your attention more."

Black said curtly, "You've had your visit. Don't come back." He waited; when Cohoon said nothing, he went on harshly: "Arroyo Street is out of bounds to your kind. Don't come this side of Main Street. It is a rule I enforce: decent citizens are entitled to some protection from the scum and riff-raff of the town. If I find you here again, I'll arrest you; and if you resist, I'll shoot you down."

Cohoon said softly, "You take your duties seriously, Willie."

"In your case, it's a pleasure," the young marshal said in the same harsh voice; then he glanced toward the lighted house up the street. "You've done her enough harm, Cohoon. You, and her own mistaken loyalty to a man who isn't good enough to enter the same room with her, the same house even! You and your family of bullies and braggarts; do you think I've forgotten that I almost drowned to give you a moment's laughter? And what are you now with the rest of them gone, Cohoon? A jailbird, a would-be thief who couldn't even carry out his part of a cheap holdup!" Black's voice broke with anger, so that for a moment he sounded very young. He caught himself, and went on: "From your expression as you left the house, I gather that she has come to her senses and sent you away. Don't try to go back, Cohoon. Leave Miss Paradine alone."

Cohoon studied the younger man for a long, tight moment; abruptly he laughed. Bill Black and the whole evening had become ridiculous.

"A badge is a handy tool for a jealous man," he murmured. "Good night, Willie." He turned away. The marshal's voice checked him.

"Cohoon, you're mistaken in what you're thinking. She barely knows I exist. I wouldn't dare to presume—"

"Why not?" Cohoon asked. "The field is clear."

"Is it?" Bill Black asked bitterly. He made a gesture, and they both stood watching the short stocky figure of Paul Westerman ascend the steps of the Paradine house. The door opened, and he went inside. Cohoon laughed softly. Even to his own ears the laughter had a wicked sound. You could ask only so much of a sense of humor. He turned and strode away without speaking, leaving the marshal still standing there.

Creek Lane was in full swing when Cohoon reached it. Entering the Double Eagle, he paused briefly inside the door to look at Francis Paradine who was sitting at a table by the wall, accompanied by some other young men and a couple of Miss Bessie's girls. Young Paradine's attitude made it clear that he was no stranger here, and that he was already well on the way to being drunk, although he could not have been here long. Cohoon grimaced; no one seemed to have gained very much by his romantic sacrifice of five years ago, not even the boy for whom, in the last analysis, the sacrifice had been made.

Miss Bessie herself was easy enough to locate at the end of the bar: a tall, spinsterish female, thin of face and body, with the clothes and demeanor of uncompromising respectability—until she laughed, which she did often. Her hearty, ribald laughter then reached into all corners of the room, despite the noise. She turned her scrutiny on Cohoon as he approached, but did not speak, leaving the initiative to him.

"I'm looking for a girl," he said.

"You'd be Boyd Cohoon," she said. "The resemblance to your brother Jonathan would be quite striking if you had another two inches and forty pounds. Did you have a particular girl in mind, Mr. Cohoon, or will anything in skirts do?"

He said, "She told me her name was Nan. Nan Montoya. There was something said about a drink on the house."

6

WHEN HE AWOKE, he was lying on a cot of sorts in a room with adobe walls. The ceiling was supported, as was customary, by evenly spaced *vigas*—peeled pine poles some five inches in diameter, serving as rafters. There was a blanket over him. His boots had been removed by whoever had brought him here. The identity of the person escaped him, in this first moment of awakening. He had got quite drunk, as had been his intention. It had been a remedy prescribed by Ward Cohoon for the times in a man's life when he discovers that he has been an outsize damn fool.

Cohoon sat up. A stout, elderly Mexican woman was crouching by the fireplace in the corner. She looked at him without favor, rose, and walked out of the room, but not before he had seen the gleam of a knife as she returned it to some hiding place among the folds of her clothing. The doorway between rooms was an arch in a thick adobe wall, closed by a blanket of Navajo design. He heard the sound of voices beyond. The woman returned and took up her position by the fire. Presently Nan Montoya came in.

"Does *despierto* mean that you're in desperate straits?" she asked, smiling. "It seems likely, considering the amount of whisky you put away last night."

Memory returned to him as he looked at her. She had exchanged last evening's finery for a plain gingham dress, but he could still in his mind see her singing to the rough crowd in the Double Eagle in a clear and accurate voice, interspersing the old-time sentimental favorites with several ballads the words of which had been, to say the least, suggestive. The contrast between her detached, almost ladylike manner, and the substance of these songs, had struck the fancy of her audience. Afterwards, noticing him with Miss Bessie at the bar, she had come to him, seeming glad to see him. Later in the evening, he recalled, there had been some kind of disturbance outside and the place had emptied. She had guided him out by a side door and brought him here—for what purpose he had been in no state to determine. Certainly there had been no romantic passages between them. Cohoon glanced at the old woman by the fire, and grinned.

"I reckon it's a good thing I don't walk in my sleep, ma'am," he said to Nan Montoya. "Your duenna packs a knife a foot long; she'd have slit my throat from ear to ear."

"Yes, isn't she a dear?" Nan said. "Miss Bessie offered me one of her upstairs rooms—I suppose there's no reason why I should set myself above the rest of the girls by refusing, but I did, so she sent me here, saying that Jesusa would protect me." The girl laughed. "I had a terrible time getting her to even let you in. *Borracho,* she kept saying, *muy borracho!* I couldn't seem to get across to her that your life was in danger."

Cohoon frowned. "In danger?"

"Why, yes," Nan said. "Miss Bessie pointed out a man she said worked for somebody named Westerman—a big, bearded, dirty-looking bully of a fellow. She said I'd better get you out of there at the first opportunity, since you were hardly in a condition to defend yourself properly. You didn't even have a gun. So when all the shooting started over on Main Street, and everybody ran out to look . . ." She shrugged her shoulders. "I still don't know what was going on. It sounded like a major battle. I didn't know anywhere else to take you, so I brought you here."

"I'm grateful," he said.

31

"Don't be," she said. "I was just returning a kindness."

"I'm only afraid you've put yourself in a bad light, ma'am," he said. "People are apt to think—"

She laughed quickly. "Cohoon, a girl who entertains in a place like the Double Eagle, whatever her duties, hasn't got a reputation to worry about. They'll think the same of me whatever I do—all those fine respectable people on the other side of your Main Street—so why shouldn't I do what I like? Tell me, what does *despierto* really mean?"

"It means 'awake,'" he said. "With a name like Montoya, you should know that much Spanish."

"The name's not mine," she said, adding in a dry voice: "I was requested not to disgrace my real one further; and Montoya was handy. As I told you yesterday, I have no legal right to it." She smiled coolly. "His first name was Raoul. Does that help me to understand French?" Then the smile vanished, and her voice sharpened: "There's something about having a man around at this hour of the morning that makes me talk too much, I guess. Your boots are by the door. There's a basin and pitcher of water at the side of the house; you can go out through the other room. Jesusa will have some coffee ready by the time you're cleaned up. Looking at you, I'd say you wouldn't be good for much more in the way of breakfast. I'm going to run over to Miss Bessie's for a moment and find out what happened last night; I'll be right back."

The other room was small and bare, furnished only with a bed, a chair, and a small brown trunk that Cohoon recognized, having seen it on the stagecoach. Some feminine garments, among them the brief and gaudy dress the girl had worn the night before, were laid out across the bed; others hung from pegs in the adobe walls. The floor was dirt, recently swept. An ornate guitar leaned in the corner. Cohoon frowned at this briefly, shrugged, and went out through the door, stripped to the waist, and washed himself thoroughly; the cold water made him feel better. When he came back into the main room of the house, the old woman put a mug of coffee into his hands.

He squatted down beside the fire to drink it, keeping his mind clear of thought. It was not yet time for thinking. He had cherished a certain picture of the future for five years, adding to it constantly, elaborating and refining it, never allowing himself to doubt it. In Yuma a man could not afford to doubt that someone was waiting to help him build his life anew when he got out. Well, he thought wryly, the belief had served its purpose; even though false, it had seen him through.

There was no hurry about making new plans; it was better just to get used to being free again, and see how things shaped up.

Nan came in, and paused to beat the dust from her skirts as Cohoon stood up.

"I must say," she said, laughing, "this is just about the dirtiest country I've lived in; I've even got it in my teeth. Does it ever stop blowing out here?"

"When it does," Cohoon said dryly, "you'll probably find the heat unbearable."

"My dear man," she said, "I've discovered that very few things are unbearable—certainly never the climate." She gave him a critical look. "Well, you look better. I will say this for you, Cohoon, when you decide to get drunk, you don't let anything stand in your way, not even an attractive woman, if I may flatter myself a bit. I found you a very dull companion last night. . . . Thanks, Jesusa." She took the cup of coffee offered her by the Mexican woman, and sat down on the cot upon which Cohoon had slept. "I seem to make a habit of being wrong about you," she murmured, regarding him across the room. "In the coach coming here, I would certainly not have taken you for a heavy drinker, any more than I could have guessed that you were a convicted stage robber. Well, I've been wrong about a man before, and I probably will be again."

He said, "I don't make a practice of drinking that much, ma'am. Last night was by way of being a celebration. I was burying a damn fool."

"Yes," she said. "I know. Miss Bessie was very informative this morning. It appears there's some doubt that the right man went to prison."

Cohoon said, "Not in the jury's mind, ma'am."

"You confessed, and the jury took you at your word, from what Miss Bessie said. She also told me certain other things. I can see how you might have felt like drinking a little too much last night. There's nothing that hurts quite as much as learning that . . . that a person who means a great deal to you has played you for a sucker, is there, Cohoon?" There was bitterness in her voice; then she smiled, getting up. "Another cup? And please stop calling me ma'am. It reminds me of when I used to teach Sunday School back home. I really did, you know. I also sang in the choir. You never know what's going to come in handy, do you?" She took the empty cup from him, hesitated, and turned back to look at him again. He was startled to see that her eyes were wet. "Cohoon, get out of

33

here," she said. "Please? You make me feel sorry for myself; I don't know why."

He nodded, and crossed the room to get his hat. At the door, he stopped. "I'm heading out for the ranch as soon as I can get an outfit together," he said. "But I'll be back in a couple of days, after I've seen what kind of shape the place is in. If you run into anything Jesusa can't handle, leave word for me at Van Houck's."

She was standing quite still by the fireplace, looking tall and slender in the low, dingy room. "Haven't you learned your lesson yet?" she asked softly. "If what I've heard about you is true, I should think you'd be cured of making romantic gestures. Just go. You don't owe me anything. . . . Oh, wait. You're forgetting something."

He frowned, uncomprehending. She went quickly into the other room; and he heard the trunk open and close. She came back with a rectangular, paper-wrapped package.

"It fell out of your pocket last night," she said. "Naturally I looked inside. It's a good thing you were under my eyes the whole time the robbery was going on, or I'd be doing some wondering this morning, after seeing that!"

"The robbery?"

"Why, yes, the office of some mining company on Main Street was robbed last night, Miss Bessie says." She smiled briefly. "The payroll they got was the one that came into town with us—remember those two rude men with that big valise?" She held out the package, glanced at it, and smiled again in a reluctant way. "You're too trusting, Cohoon. It's not fair to put so much temptation in a girl's way. Why, with half of what's in there—a quarter, even—I could go away and renounce this life of shame forever."

He looked at the package for a moment, and at the girl who held it. "Take it all," he said.

Her eyes widened. "That's a cruel joke. It would serve you right if I took you up on it."

"Go ahead," he said. "In case you should have doubts, the money was honestly come by. You might even say I earned it."

She looked at him steadily. "I see," she breathed at last. "What Miss Bessie told me was right then. The girl's name was Paradine," she said. And when you came back, after doing that for her, she had her father pay you off in money! I can see why you needed a drink or two last night."

Cohoon said, "Miss Bessie talks too much."

"But why give it to me?" Nan asked. "What are you buying, Cohoon?"

"Miss Bessie talks too much," Cohoon said, "and for a girl with ten thousand dollars in her hand, you're asking a lot of questions, ma'am."

She studied his face a moment longer, and laughed curtly. "All right," she said. "I think I understand. You're buying revenge, aren't you? Very well, I'll do my best to give it to you. At the price, I can't afford to refuse."

7

WHEN SHE came out of the kitchen after supervising the final details of breakfast, Claire Paradine was surprised to find her brother already seated at the dining table—although "seated" was too kind a word for his posture, she reflected, since he was slumped forward on his elbows and sipping noisily from a coffee cup held in both hands.

"Put the platter down there, Teresa," she said in Spanish to the maid who had followed her. "And you can call Colonel Paradine now. . . . Francis, do you have to drink like that?" she asked in English.

The boy looked up at her. His eyes were bloodshot, and there was a hint of blond stubble on his chin—she could never get over a faint sense of shock upon having it called to her attention that her baby brother was old enough to shave. It reminded her harshly of her own age. *Why, I'm a spinster,* she thought, *soon they'll be calling me an old maid.*

Francis said, "Yes, dear sister, I do have to drink in this manner, since unfortunately my condition precludes my holding the cup steady in any other way. Precludes is a nice word, isn't it? We Paradines know a great many nice words. I'm not the only person whose hand is shaking this morning, Claire. What nice words did you use on Boyd Cohoon last night?"

She said quickly, "That's none of your—"

"Oh, but it is my business," Francis said. "Since, afterwards, your victim made himself and his frame of mind very conspicuous. He came into my favorite place of relaxation and proceeded to drink himself unconscious in a most systematic manner, in the company of one of the entertainers—quite a pretty wench, too. For reasons you'll appreciate, I didn't stay to watch the whole unpleasant performance."

Claire said stiffly, "I'm not the least bit interested in hearing how Mr. Cohoon spends his time; but your attitude toward him is unseemly, Francis, considering what he did for you."

35

The boy looked up quickly; and she was startled by the sudden malevolence of his expression. Of late there were times when he seemed an adult and not very likeable stranger.

"Don't ever say that!" he told her in a tight, strained voice. "I never asked any favors of Boyd Cohoon. What he did, he did for you, not for me."

She said, shocked, "Why, you hate him!"

"Wouldn't you? If you'd spent five years listening to whispers and insinuations. . . . Do you think people don't know what actually happened five years ago? Sometimes I think everybody in town knows it except your friend Westerman with his determined hatred for Cohoon—and sometimes I even wonder about him. He must have heard the story somewhere; he hears everything else that happens. I wouldn't be surprised to learn that he knows perfectly well who really held up the stage with Harry that day, and just pretends to think it was Cohoon for some sly reason of his own."

Claire felt a pang of fear. "Now you're being ridiculous! Unless . . . You haven't said anything in front of him that would lead him to suspect, have you?"

Her brother laughed. "Do you think I'm a fool? Even if I didn't care about my own skin, I wouldn't dream of spoiling your little game, and Dad's. How much is Dad into him for, anyway?"

"I don't know what you mean," Claire said stiffly.

"Dad knows about as much about silver and mining as I do," Francis said. "A clever man could take him for every penny he owned—unless there was something he wanted more than pennies." The boy laughed again. "We're quite a gang of slave traders, aren't we, Claire? You pay off my debt to society with Boyd Cohoon's body, and Dad pays off his debt to Paul Westerman with yours, and Paul—"

"Paul what?"

"Never mind. Just a little secret of Paul's and mine."

"You're being ridiculous *and* disgusting," Claire said angrily. "I think you're drunk. And if you've been borrowing money from Paul, I'll—"

Francis chuckled. "Claire, don't threaten me. You play your game and I'll play mine. . . . Incidentally, I saw our stiff-necked marshal outside again last night; seems he's developing the habit of patrolling Arroyo Street. Sometimes I wish I'd been born a woman; it must be pleasant to be able to get what you want with no more than a smile—and a promise you don't have to keep." He rose abruptly. "As for Boyd Cohoon, of course I hate him. He's the martyred hero everyone admires;

36

while I'm the precious little fellow who stayed safe at home while another man went to prison in his place. Can I tell them that I wasn't asked; that I was out of my head from shock and loss of blood; that I didn't even know what had happened until after the trial?"

She was tired of his hints and insinuations, and she said sharply, "I did what I thought was best, and so did Dad. There was nothing to prevent you from going to the authorities as soon as you were well, and getting Boyd released, if you didn't like it."

Her brother swung to face her so quickly that for an instant she thought he would strike her, and it may have been in his mind. Then the violence seemed to drain out of him.

"Yes," he said wearily. "Thank you for reminding me, Claire. There's always that, isn't there; five years of it? I'll try not to forget it again."

She watched him stumble out of the room, regretting what she had said, although his behavior had certainly invited a little plain speaking. Then her father was coming into the room. From his carefully controlled expression she knew that he had stopped at her mother's door, as was his habit, and had as usual received no response to his morning greeting. This was a pattern she had known almost all her life. She could remember very clearly when it started. She had been a child then, and Francis had been a baby, too young to understand. The evening had been much the same as any other; at dinner, her mother had voiced her customary complaints about this country and its climate, fit only for the savages to whom it really belonged. The children had been put to bed; but Claire had been awakened some hours later by angry voices in the adjoining room. Her mother was laying down an ultimatum: she and the children were going back to Virginia; her father could suit himself. Then she heard her father's voice, the voice of a man driven beyond endurance, explaining in cold hard words, intelligible even to a four-year-old child, exactly why they had left home immediately after the war, and why they could never go back.

She had never been able to look at her father since without remembering that night. Now she watched him come to the table with the same emotions as always: love and pity and— she could not help it—a little contempt, because of course he had tried to justify himself in the end.

"What's the matter with Francis?" Colonel Paradine asked.

Claire said, "He's disturbed because Boyd Cohoon got publicly drunk last night after leaving us." She hesitated.

37

"Maybe . . . maybe I should have been nicer to him. After all—"

"No, no, my dear, you did just right." The Colonel continued to speak in a measured way as they seated themselves at the table. "I really think you gave young Cohoon all the consideration he deserved in putting off your marriage until you could break the news to him. And what with the not inconsiderable sum he received in addition, I can't see that he has any cause for complaint." He spread his napkin, and caressed his pale mustache with a forefinger. "I must say, my dear, that I'm very relieved with the way this has turned out. There was a time when I feared you were becoming emotionally involved with that young fellow; and the Cohoon men were always a rough lot, Claire. Why, Ward Cohoon carried half a dozen scalps at his belt for years after he settled here, and a tomahawk as well, having lived with the eastern tribes in his youth, before he crossed the plains. It's a mystery why Mrs. Cohoon, an educated woman of good family, allowed herself to be practically abducted by a wild man in buckskin who, according to the stories I've heard, made no bones whatever about having come back east just to find himself a wife. Perhaps she was influenced by the fact that, unlike most of those frontiersmen, he had managed to make quite a bit of money; but I have no doubt that she regretted her choice before she died." Colonel Paradine dismissed the Cohoons with a gesture. "Well," he said cheerily, "I suppose we can start making plans for the wedding, now that your conscience is satisfied. Did you and Paul agree on a date last night?"

"No," he said. "No, we didn't. I didn't feel . . . I was a little upset. Seeing Boyd again . . ." Her voice trailed away.

Her father cleared his throat, and said, "Claire, I'd like to remind you that according to the laws of this territory you can marry only one man. I'd also like to point out that I'm involved in some fairly important business dealings with Paul Westerman. I don't mention this as an argument for marrying him—I've left the decision entirely up to you, haven't I, my dear?—but I think I have the right to insist that you treat him with consideration. He's been very patient with these delays; I certainly hope he doesn't connect them with young Cohoon. He certainly deserves a straightforward answer now."

She said, "I know. Paul's been sweet." She toyed with the food on her plate, and spoke again without looking up: "Dad, how important is it to you that I marry him?"

The Colonel glanced at her quickly, and looked quickly away. "Important?" he said in a carefully even voice. "Why,

I don't know what you mean, my dear. As I've said time and again, the decision is entirely up to you. I only want your happiness, you know that." After a moment, he added easily, "But surely you're not thinking of refusing him, after keeping him waiting this long?" Then, as if feeling that he had betrayed himself, he added in an altogether different tone: "Well, I'd better get to the bank, my dear. Let me know what you decide."

"I'll come with you, if you don't mind, Dad," Claire said. "I want to do some shopping later, and there's no money in the house."

Outside, it was blowing hard, so that it was a relief when they reached their destination and the doors closed against the dust and sand. Entering the bank with her father was always a pleasure to Claire Paradine; it was rather like being a princess inspecting the household troops. She smiled at the guard, and the Mexican boy who was sweeping the floor, and at the two tellers—giving a special smile to young John Fergus, who was in love with her. Francis, she noted, had not yet arrived for work. Inside the rear office, the Colonel paused to leaf through some papers left on the desk for his inspection.

"Just sit down for a minute, my dear," he said. "I'll be right . . . Yes, what is it, Fergus?"

The young teller stood in the doorway with an odd expression on his freckled face. He glanced at Claire—a look of acute embarrassment—hesitated, flushed, and addressed her father:

"If you don't mind, I'd like to speak to you privately, sir."

"What . . . Oh, very well."

The Colonel walked across the room; Fergus followed him outside. They did not close the door. Claire, from where she sat, could hear the younger man's subdued voice; she saw her father's back stiffen. Without looking around, the Colonel followed Fergus toward the front of the bank. Claire sat for a moment motionless; then, drawn by an uneasy curiosity she could not control, she rose and moved to the open door.

She heard her father's voice, peculiarly strained, say, "Yes, yes, of course we'll be glad to open an account for Mrs. Montoya."

Then she saw the person to whom her father was speaking; a rather tall, dark-haired girl in an elaborate, shiny green dress, and a large feathered hat that no respectable woman would have dreamed of wearing. But it was not the female's costume that held Claire Paradine's shocked attention, but

39

what the creature held in her hand: a rectangular packet, the proportions and wrappings of which were horribly familiar. She knew a quick and bitter hatred for Boyd Cohoon, who had taken this brutal way of expressing his opinion of the Paradines' money—throwing it casually to this hussy in payment, no doubt, for a night's favors.

"Ten thousand dollars," Colonel Paradine said thickly. His neck was red with suppressed fury. "Yes, of course, Mrs. Montoya. We are here to serve the public."

8

STANDING at the rear of the store where Van Houck kept his stock of firearms, Cohoon buckled the heavy revolver about him, adjusting the weapon on his left hip, butt forward, where it could be reached with either hand. His father had often spoken caustically of the kind of barroom desperadoes who packed their guns down about their knees and could, as a consequence, barely hobble across the sidewalk into the nearest saloon. Van Houck made change for a female customer, and came back along the aisle.

"Stop licking your chops, Uncle Van," Cohoon said. "I'm not going after Westerman; I'm just putting this damn thing on so I won't look naked walking around town. It might put notions into somebody's head."

Van Houck said, "You sound like your dad. He used to say that a gun without a man was a useless hunk of iron; while a man without a gun was still a man." After a moment's pause, he went on: "I'm sorry if I spoke harshly yesterday, Boyd. It is not my place to tell you what to do. If I believed strongly enough that the fellow should be shot, I should go shoot him myself, *hein?* Maybe I will, if his fine new place across the street continues to lure my customers away."

Cohoon laughed. "If you want to shoot him for that, okay!" he said. "But before you shoot him for Dad and Jonathan, you'd better make sure you have the right man."

"What do you mean?"

Cohoon hesitated. "You told me they couldn't find the marshal that day when the posse was being formed, so they rode without him, Westerman taking the lead. . . ."

"I doubt they looked very hard, Boyd. Westerman likes to run things his own way; and since they pinned a badge on

40

young Black he's been acting pretty independent. Westerman wouldn't have wanted him along, particularly if there might be some evidence to be concealed." Van Houck chuckled. "To look at the boy now, dressed like every day was Sunday, you wouldn't think that only a few years ago he was well on the way to becoming just another drunken bum like his dad. After the new bridge put the ferry out of business, he got a job in Flagler's place on Creek Lane and showed himself to be pretty handy with a gun—also with a bottle. Everybody was saying that the kid was the spitting image of old John Black, particularly when he was full of whisky. He's got a mean streak in him, just like the old man. . . ."

Cohoon said dryly, "What man doesn't? But with that kind of a reputation, how did he manage to get chosen marshal?"

"Well, it was a matter of finding someone who could handle the job; and he could do that, all right. And then it was also a matter of getting a man who'd keep this mining riffraff from taking over the town; and whatever you may say against John Black, he *was* one of the old settlers: his son could be counted on not to side with the newcomers. And I guess Westerman, who was behind the Citizens' Committee, figured that with his drinking he'd be easy enough to handle. However, that was one time Paul Westerman figured wrong. The idea that a bunch of his fellow-citizens thought enough of him to put the law into his hands did something for young Black; I guess nobody ever trusted him with anything before. He took his new job seriously, as you can see. A little too seriously for the liking of some people—why is it that reforming a man always makes him insufferably righteous?—but I wish him luck. After the way Old John used to abuse him while he was alive, the boy deserves a break now."

Cohoon said, "Perhaps. Nevertheless, I'd be interested in knowing just where he was that day he couldn't be found. The day Dad and Jonathan were killed."

Van Houck looked up quickly, startled. "Boyd, you don't think—"

"Last night Willie Black came as close as a man could come to expressing delight that the rest of my family was no longer living, which is odd behavior for a righteous man, Uncle Van."

"Ah, he always carried a grudge against Jonathan for some boyhood joke, I know that; but it never occurred to me . . . What are you going to do?"

"Do?" Cohoon said. "Why, I'm going to do nothing along those lines, just as I have been doing. I told you last night that

41

I can stand having the murderer around; I've got other business besides playing detective. But I still wonder, Uncle Van, just how long he can stand having me around. It will be interesting to see how long his nerve holds out, eh, Uncle Van?" Cohoon picked up his hat. "Well, I'll lug this saddle and gear up the street and see if I can't swindle Ben Swanson out of a horse and pack mule for old times' sake. I'll pick up the rest of the outfit on the way back."

Outside, he had to narrow his eyes against the sunshine and dust—in some parts of the world, people wrote odes to spring, but around here it was a time of high winds and flying dirt. A woman near the hotel was having trouble maintaining her skirts at a decorous level; and a tumbleweed came bouncing down the center of Main Street. Cohoon walked up the street, passing the bank; he paused to look at a building a little farther on, across the front of which was lettered: LUCKY SEVEN MINING CO. The windows were shattered and the walls pockmarked by recent gunfire. As Cohoon stood there, Marshal Black came out of the place and, seeing him, walked up to him.

"Where were you?" the marshal asked, glancing at the bullet-marked walls.

"Not here," Cohoon said, catching his meaning, which was clear enough.

Black said: "You rode into town with this money, Cohoon. It was taken the evening you arrived. That's a coincidence, and I don't like coincidences. *Somebody* sent word to the General that a big payroll had been slipped by him, bringing him here last night to remedy the oversight."

"The General?" Cohoon let the heavy saddle slide from his shoulder, and lowered it to the ground.

"Of course, you wouldn't know about the General," Black said sarcastically. "He's only been operating in this country the last three-four years; and nobody could possibly have told you how to get in touch with him—one of your fellow-convicts, perhaps, with some helpful suggestions for finding employment after your release?" The marshal laughed sharply. "I know crooks, and how information passes among them, Cohoon. My dad was one, remember? He was better than you; he made more money and he never got caught. But once a man goes bad, a few years in prison won't cure him—and you're one of the bad ones."

Cohoon said softly, "According to the law, which you're supposed to enforce, I've paid my debt to society."

The younger man looked at him thoughtfully, ignoring his

words. "I don't think you were planted on the stage," he said, in the tones of one who speculates aloud. "I think you just had a lucky break—according to your point of view—and took advantage of it. Broke, just out of prison, you had some valuable information dropped in your lap; and if you didn't already know where to locate a buyer for it, you found out in a hurry. The General's got spies in town; we know that from the way he operates. For a man with your record it would have been no problem at all to get in touch with him. . . . That's a nice-looking saddle, Cohoon. And a new gun, too."

"On credit," Cohoon said. "Ask Van Houck."

"He'd lie for you. It was a mistake, Cohoon. On your part *and* that of the General. He should have stuck to holding up stagecoaches and harassing the outlying mines. He shouldn't have committed a robbery in my town, and you shouldn't have helped him. Tell him that, Cohoon, the next time you see him."

The words had an amusing overtone of hurt boyish pride; but the young marshal's expression was less amusing. After a moment longer, Black turned abruptly and walked away in the direction of his office, located beyond the hotel. Cohoon watched him briefly, and bent down to pick up the saddle on the ground.

"Cohoon."

He glanced up to see Paul Westerman standing in the doorway of the mine office, in his shirt sleeves. Cohoon lowered the saddle again, and walked over.

"So young Black suspects you of having a hand in the robbery," Westerman said. "It's a thought that hadn't occurred to me."

Cohoon shrugged. He looked through the doorway, seeing a desk at which a clerk was working, and an open safe. He looked back at Westerman. "Yours?"

"The Lucky Seven? Yes, it's one of my enterprises. We're just adding up our losses—subtracting them, I guess I should say." Westerman grimaced ruefully. "Overconfidence, Cohoon. We thought we'd been very clever to get the payroll into town without being noticed, and left only two men to guard the safe. They were expecting no trouble, since the General's never struck in town before—we were all preparing ourselves for the real job of getting the money out to the mine tomorrow. He simply outwitted us, as he has a habit of doing."

Cohoon asked, "Who is he, Mr. Westerman?"

"The General? The man who knows the answer to that is in a fair way to earning himself the reward, which I have just doubled, making it two thousand dollars." Westerman shrugged. "Oh, we know something about him, of course. He's supposed to have come across the border two jumps ahead of the *rurales;* I guess he'd tried his hand at revolution down there like most of those fellows. That was four years ago; now he's got himself a gang of outlaws—Mexicans and renegade Apaches mostly—and has settled down to live comfortably off the Americanos. He wears a fancy uniform and hides out in the *malpais* to the north. You know that country; you can see how much chance a posse of citizens has of catching a gang of twenty-thirty armed outlaws in that mess of black rock." Westerman shook his head. "We don't even try any more, as you can see. The last posse got itself pretty badly shot up when it pushed the General a little too hard—he doesn't mind being followed, that's part of the game, but he considers it impolite of us to step on his heels. No, the General himself has become pretty much a natural phenomenon as far as we're concerned, like the weather. The fellow we're really after is the man here in town who supplies him with his information. If we ever find that man, there are going to be a lot of angry citizens ready to stretch his neck in a quick and final way, Cohoon. You might keep that in mind."

Cohoon said, "If this General's been operating for four years, I've got a pretty good alibi."

"Maybe. But people aren't very reasonable when they're aroused. If they find a man who passed information to the General today, they aren't going to worry about the fact that he couldn't have done it yesterday."

"I thank you for the warning, Mr. Westerman," Cohoon said.

"I gave you another warning, Boyd. There'll be a stage south the day after tomorrow. Be on it. Or find a horse to put under that saddle and head out of here today."

They looked at each other for a silent moment; then Cohoon grinned and walked off without speaking. There was, after all, no sense in making the older man a present of his intentions, when keeping quiet might keep trouble off his neck for a day or two longer.

Ben Swanson greeted him warmly—a tall, bald and bony man who had not changed in appearance in the two decades Cohoon had known him.

"This is a fine new place I have here, eh?" he said, showing Cohoon around. "Sold my other place to some fool from the east to build a store on. If I don't take his money somebody else get it. Bunch of crazy people all thinking they get rich

44

tomorrow. Pretty soon somebody find silver or gold somewhere else and they all go away. Let them go. I still have my new stables, eh? Like your dad used to say, digging holes in the ground is for rodents, not men." He clapped Cohoon on the shoulder. "Sorry about your dad. He was a fine man. I've got a nice bay gelding back here I'll give you cheap for his memory, and throw a mule in for nothing."

"What's wrong with the mule?" Cohoon asked.

"Everything's wrong with the mule," Swanson said. "It's the meanest damn mule I ever laid eyes on, but what do you care? For nothing you can afford to shoot him when you can't stand his cussedness any longer. . . ."

It was pleasant to be astride a horse again. Cohoon rode down Main Street at an easy gait, swearing occasionally at the mule, which already showed promise of living up to Swanson's description. As he neared the bank, a woman in a green dress emerged and crossed the street ahead of him, using one hand to control her skirts and the other to maintain her hat upon her head. She paused in the lee of the buildings, and he recognized her, and reined in as he came abreast of the spot. After a moment Nan became aware of him, and looked up, coming to the edge of the boardwalk.

"You look better on a horse, Cohoon," she said. She reached out a cautious hand. "Do I pat him, or will he bite me? My experience with horses has been limited to a Boston bridlepath."

"The horse is all right, I reckon, but stay clear of the mule; he's supposed to be mean." He hooked a knee over the horn, looking down at her critically. "You're all dressed up for a party," he said.

She smiled. "The party's over; and your money's in the bank. I dressed up for the occasion, thinking you'd want me to look the part I was playing."

"Your money," he said.

"As you wish." She smiled again, a little crookedly. "You'll be pleased to know that the girl was there when I made the deposit. I wouldn't have thought that fragile blonde type would appeal to you; but then, as I said this morning, I've made mistakes about men before. She would have loved to scratch my eyes out. Her father looked as if he'd swallowed a bad egg. It's too bad you couldn't have watched, Cohoon, since you're paying high for the revenge."

He said, "Aren't you jumping to conclusions, ma'am?"

"Am I?" She shook her head quickly. "I don't think so. You could just have refused the money, couldn't you? Or,

45

having taken it, you could have given it to the church, if you couldn't bring yourself to spend it. Or thrown it into the arroyo. But you wanted to strike back at her, to hurt her, so you handed it to me, knowing the conclusions she would draw when she heard of it. Well, you can feel satisfied. She's thinking just what you wanted her to think, and no one can blame her. Why else would a man toss such a pack of bank notes to a dance-hall entertainer? So I feel that I have earned my pay, Cohoon. It was a little distasteful, but a girl in my position can't afford to be choosy. Any time you have more money to dispose of in the same way, why, drop around. I'll be glad to handle it for you."

There was anger and some contempt in her voice; and he knew a quick regret: he had repaid her badly for her kindness of the night before. Giving her the money had been an impulsive gesture; superficially he had meant no harm, but she had read accurately the deeper, ugly motives of which he had hardly been aware.

"I'm sorry, ma'am," he said. "I apologize. To you. Not to her."

After a moment, she smiled. "You seem to have a habit of going off half-cocked, as they say out here, don't you, Cohoon? And please stop calling me ma'am; I've asked you that before. . . . Well, I think we've given the natives enough to talk about for one morning, and I've got to run over a few songs with the piano player. Drop in and hear them when you get back to town."

He raised his hat as she turned away; and watched her move down the street serenely, as if unconscious of the interested and critical glances that followed her. She turned right at Creek Lane. He kicked his horse into motion and rode down as far as Van Houck's, where he packed his outfit on the reluctant mule. Leaving the animals there, he walked across the street to the hotel, to pick up the belongings in his room. When he stopped at the desk on his way out, the clerk was speaking to a young man in eastern clothes, rather dusty from traveling.

"No, sir," the clerk said, "we have no lady of that description staying here. What did you say the name was?"

"Wyatt," the young man said. "Miss Nancy Wyatt. I'm very anxious to get in touch with her; in fact I rode an empty ore wagon up rather than wait for the next stagecoach. You'd know her if you saw her; she's a rather striking . . . well, you'd know her. I've traced her clear from San Francisco. . . ."

He broke off, becoming aware of Cohoon's presence. The clerk looked up.

"Oh, Mr. Cohoon," he said, and moved over to take care of the bill. The transaction finished, Cohoon hesitated for a moment, looking at the easterner, who looked pale and downy and very young. After five years in jail, Cohoon had discovered, every man his own age looked callow and immature; and back east they grew up even more slowly than they did out here. This was a boy; a boy with romantic notions who had apparently followed a dream several thousand miles west around the continent to San Francisco, and another thousand miles back south and east again to Arizona territory and, after all that traveling, his dream still bright, had been unable to wait an extra day or two for the stage but had jumped aboard the first ore wagon headed north. . . . Cohoon turned on his heel and walked away. He had gone a long way for a dream once, himself, and had discovered for himself what dreams were worth. Besides, the business of playing Good Samaritan had proved fairly unprofitable to date.

9

WILLIAM BLACK studied his visitor without enthusiasm: these easterners had notions about the law and its enforcement that were far removed from western realities.

He said, "Sit down, Mr. James. What's the trouble?"

The young man sat down stiffly and placed his hat on his lap. "Well," he said, "the clerk over at the hotel said you might be able to help me, Marshal. I'm looking for a girl."

Black laughed briefly. "That's a common complaint, Mr. James. You'd be surprised how many miners come into this town of a Saturday night with the same. . . ." His visitor showed no trace of a smile; and the marshal checked himself, a little annoyed at the failure of his attempt at humor, particularly since he was aware that the subject was nothing for decent men to joke about. "The young lady's name?" he said curtly.

"Wyatt," said the boy from the east. "Nancy Wyatt."

"Can you give me a description?"

"Why, yes. She's fairly tall, slender, dark-haired and . . . and beautiful."

"Color of eyes?"

"Gray," James said. "Greenish gray."

"Would you have a picture of her, Mr. James?"

"Why, yes," said James, and produced a small, flat leather case which, opened, revealed a photographic print, ovally framed. "This was taken three years ago," he said. "We . . . we were about to be married."

Black turned the picture around and studied it for a moment. A hint of recognition stirred in his mind.

"You were to be married?" he said after a moment. "Then I presume this is not a criminal matter, merely a personal one. The young lady hasn't committed any—"

"Of course not!"

"Then," the marshal said, "the matter is somewhat outside my jurisdiction, Mr. James. However—"

"Yes?"

"Leaving the law out of it," Black said, "I can offer some advice, which you are free to take or leave as you see fit."

"Yes?"

"If I were you, Mr. James," Black said evenly, "I would go back home."

The youth looked up quickly, startled. He said, "You do know something about Nancy! You've seen her!"

Black put his fingernail against the photograph and pushed it gently across the desk. "You say this picture was made three years ago. I reckon the young lady disappeared from wherever she lived—"

"Boston."

"—disappeared from Boston about that time?"

"It was about six months later, three days before the . . ." James checked himself.

Black said, "Two and a half years. People can change in two and a half years, Mr. James."

James got to his feet abruptly. "I don't know what you're trying to say, and I don't care to hear it! Where is she, Marshal? All I want to know is where to find her!"

Black stared across the desk; he would, he told himself, have liked to spare the youth in front of him—actually no younger than himself—but it would have been a mistaken kindness.

"I can't be sure from the picture, Mr. James," he said. "However, a young lady of that general description did arrive on the stagecoach yesterday, in the company of an unsavory character named Cohoon, just freed after serving a five-year term in the Territorial Prison for armed robbery."

James winced. "Cohoon?" he said. "I've heard that name.

Is he about my own size, a lean, dark-haired fellow with a pale complexion? He came through the hotel lobby—"

"That's the man. One of our picturesque Western characters, Mr. James; and I might add, a thoroughly unpleasant and dangerous person despite his mild looks. That's why I suggested it might be better if you returned home."

"And you suggest that Nancy is . . . is associated with this . . . badman?"

"She arrived in town with him," Black said. "He took her directly to one of our more colorful local establishments, where she is now working as entertainer. She lives in a house off Creek Lane, alone except for a Mexican woman—and Mr. Cohoon, when he chooses to take advantage of her hospitality, as he did last night."

"You're lying!" James cried.

Black leaned forward slightly. "Mr. James, out here it's not considered polite to question another man's truthfulness. You asked for information and I'm giving it to you. That Cohoon spent the night in the Montoya girl's house is a fact which I can bring witnesses to prove."

"Montoya?" James said. "Is that what she calls herself?"

"Nan Montoya. Do you recognize the name? She also, I'm given to understand, at the first opportunity deposited in the bank a large sum of money which she seems to have received from him—I'm trying to learn the source of that money. It seems quite a coincidence that we should have a robbery in town within four hours of Mr. Cohoon's arrival, and that his girl should make a trip to the bank the following morning. . . . What did you say, Mr. James?"

James licked his lips. "Just tell me where to find her," he whispered.

Black told him, and watched him retrieve his photograph and move toward the door with a slight feeling of shame; perhaps he had let his dislike of Cohoon cause him to paint the picture too black. Yet to the best of his knowledge he had said nothing that was not true—and it *was* odd that the girl should have opened a bank account this morning, right after Cohoon had claimed to be so broke that he had to buy his saddle on credit. . . .

49

10

THE ROAD LED across the greasewood plains in a northwesterly direction from Sombrero, past the great balanced rock that had given the town its name. There was no real need, on horseback, to follow the road, and it added some distance to the journey, but Cohoon was in no hurry, and he felt a desire, perhaps sentimental, to pass all the landmarks of his boyhood in their proper order. Four miles out of town, he paused at the junction with the old road from the south.

This had once been the main trail into this part of the country, crossing the rugged Candelaria Mountains by way of Coyote Pass, and the river at Yellow Ford. But it had never been easy for wheeled vehicles, and when John Black—whose drinking had not dulled a shrewd eye for business—had put in his ferry thirty miles to the east, traffic had shifted in that direction, swinging around the shoulder of the Candelarias, and altogether avoiding the ancient ford with its quicksands and frequent high water. Since that time, the old trail over the mountain had fallen into disuse, and the portion of it between the Diamond C and this point had served only to help the Cohoons and their riders on the way to town, saving them a long ride east across the ranch to the new road and a toll at Black's Ferry.

Under the circumstances, there should have been no traffic over it of any significance for the past two years, and perhaps there had not been. The recent hoofprints could indicate only a few casual travelers or prospectors. The most interesting signs in the dusty ground were quite old. Yet at some time since he had last been over this road, Cohoon saw, heavy wagons had used it for a considerable period of time, long enough to cut deep ruts that wind and sand—and the scant rain of this country—had not yet obliterated. The marks were deeper and wider than any ranch vehicle would leave, no matter how heavily loaded. Cohoon frowned thoughtfully, dismounted, and walked a little distance along the tracks, stopping to pick up a chunk of gray granitic rock that had obviously neither been broken nor brought here by nature. It looked to his inexpert eye like the rock that formed the core of the Candelarias, exposed on the higher slopes: but it contained veins of a darker material.

Cohoon tossed the rock aside; he knew little about prospecting and mining. In fact, he tended to share his father's notion that there was something faintly indecent about ripping the earth apart for the sake of an inanimate and relatively useless metal. Not that his father had sneered at gold or silver as a medium of exchange; he had simply had an old-fashioned notion that riches should be earned, not found. . . . In any case it seemed that, at some time since Cohoon had gone to prison five years ago, ore had been hauled this way, presumably from a mine on the near north slopes of the Candelarias, since the road led nowhere else that an ore wagon could go. At a more recent date, but still not yesterday, the traffic had stopped, at least by this route.

It was hot in the sun; Cohoon wiped out the band of his hat and took a sparing drink from the water bottle before swinging into the saddle again. He saw more scattered ore fragments along the deeply cut ruts as he rode on to the south. They disturbed him, as did the changed aspect of the road; even here, it seemed, nothing had remained the same. Only the red and orange mesas to the west and the gray-green mountains ahead looked as he remembered them.

He reached the river a little before noon and made a small fire. It was pleasant to be alone, responsible to no one but himself. After eating, he took the broken Henry rifle from his bedroll, and a strip of rawhide, which he soaked until it was soft and flexible, after which he used it to splice the stock carefully. The rawhide, drying, would shrink up tight.

He cleaned the gun—dusty from two years of idleness—checked the action, loaded the weapon, and shoved it into the saddle scabbard, after which he packed up again, and headed across the ford. The threatening rumble of the rapids upstream reached him clearly. Looking to the left, he could see the yellow torrent pouring out of the canyon, spreading out into shallows that looked innocent enough—but near the south bank of the ford he passed the remnants of a large ore wagon that had bogged down in one of the numerous shifting potholes that had always plagued this crossing. It seemed a strange thing: here, where water was more precious than silver and gold, this river had never been anything but a menace and an obstruction.

To the south, the road climbed upward through a steep canyon that cut back through the yellow cliffs. Halfway up, Cohoon checked his horse; below him on the canyon floor—

if the bottom of the narrow cleft could be so called—was the wreckage of a wagon that had apparently gone out of control on the grade. He could make out the dried, skeletal carcasses of the mules. Perhaps the driver was down there too, or perhaps he had jumped in time. Somebody must have wanted silver badly, Cohoon reflected, to try hauling it out this way. It had always been a bad enough trip with a buckboard, as he recalled, let alone with a wagon bearing several tons of ore.

He started to ride on, but checked himself and dismounted instead, tying the animals in the shadow of the overhanging cliff. Then he moved out to the edge of the road, from which he could look straight down the canyon to the ford. He squatted there in the sunshine, absently forming a cigarette with his fingers, lighting and smoking it. Presently he saw a rider, followed by two others, come down to the river from the north and make the crossing. At the distance it was hard to tell with certainty, but he thought the man in the lead had a beard. He remembered that a bearded man had tried to pick a fight with him within half an hour of his arrival in Sombrero. According to Nan Montoya, a bearded man identified by Miss Bessie as an employee of Westerman had been stalking him in the Double Eagle later the same evening, while he had been busy getting drunk. Of course, this was by no means a cleanshaven country; and it could be merely a coincidence that a bewhiskered individual was coming up the road behind him now. . . .

He walked over to his horse, and lifted the rifle out of the scabbard far enough to examine the splice he had made; it looked strong enough to stand the shock of recoil should shooting become necessary. He pushed the gun back into place, with some reluctance: this was a fine place for an ambush, and considerations of strategy indicated that it might be well to reduce the odds against him here, rather than fight in a less advantageous place later on. Yet the fact was that he could not afford to fight. A man with a prison record did not dare to kill; and any fighting in which guns were involved entailed the risk of killing no matter how carefully the shooting was done.

He dropped his cigarette, trod it out, and mounted, feeling a certain bitterness at the circumstances that would not let him make this pilgrimage in peace—but it had been a sentimental idea, after all, and he rode on at a faster pace. At the top, however, he reined in without conscious thought. He had almost forgotten the view that would greet him here; or perhaps he had been afraid to remember, afraid that this, too, would have changed. But it had not changed; and he sat for a space of minutes looking at the rolling grasslands ahead, sweeping up like a golden wave—tinged with the green of spring—toward the formidable wall of the Candelarias, twenty miles to the south.

It was a kind of homecoming, and he could see it all clearly in his mind, even the parts that were beyond the immediate range of his vision. The Grant was roughly rectangular in shape, bounded on the north by the deep and winding canyon of the river and its adjoining badlands, on the south by the mountains, and on east and west by the new road and the old. Now that there was no longer a question of a ferry toll, you could take either road north to Sombrero and beyond. The choice would depend mainly on which end of the Grant you happened to start from. Going south, however, you would be well advised to ride across to pick up the new road, even from this end of the Grant, unless you had a sure-footed horse and enjoyed the rough going over the Candelarias.

It was a good location, Cohoon reflected, and it would become better as the country became more settled, and the land itself was good. Presently he cleared his throat, and spoke aloud, although there was no one to hear.

"Well," he said, "well, I reckon it looks like we've still got the grass. Now let's see if there's any stock left to feed on it."

Suddenly eager to have this over with, he kicked the horse into motion and slashed at the recalcitrant mule, heading for home. When he reached it, the ranch house looked like any of the adobe ruins that dotted this country, marking places where people had once lived. The massive, blackened walls were still standing; you could see that it had been a somewhat larger and more elaborate house than the average—once it had been the hacienda of the Candelarias, the original owners of the Grant.

Cohoon stopped in the weed-grown yard, but did not dismount; curiously, the destruction before him meant nothing in that moment. A house was nothing without the people, and he had already resigned himself to the people being gone. It was not, after all, as if he was bringing a bride home today. . . . He spat, as if to dispose of the unwanted thought, and rode slowly ahead. With the new bridge in, he told himself, there was no longer any reason for living at this end of the Grant: all that was important here was the water tank, which would have to be cleaned out. For the cabin he had in mind, there was a location over to the east by Willow Spring that was more suitable in every respect for a ranch head-quarters.

A sound in the brush nearby brought him around with a start, to see a cow and calf break cover like deer and head up the slope away from him. On an impulse, he dropped the mule's lead rope and headed after them, cutting the horse hard for a burst of speed that brought him alongside the cow. He looked for the brand, and it was there.

It gave him a strange feeling of release to see it; and he knew that he was home after being away too long. A man tended to lose his bearings, too long away from home. Too many houses and people were confusing. You had to come back and see your own grass stretching as far as you could see, and your own brand on the side of a healthy animal, to know where you belonged.

He checked the horse, letting the cow pull ahead. It disappeared over the ridge, the calf following. He watched them go, and so became aware of the small cloud of dust that hung against the Candelaria foothills, moving slowly to the left. He studied it for about a minute, turned back and recaptured the mule after a brief chase, and headed toward the mountains at a deliberate jog trot. As the country opened up to him again, on the other side of the ridge above the burned-out ranch, he saw the new road where there had been no road before, and the two heavily laden ore wagons lumbering steadily eastward. Presently he was close enough to read the markings on their sides: *Lucky Seven Mining Co.*

The picture was suddenly quite clear in his mind. His father would never have given permission to haul ore across the Grant, certainly not to any company belonging to Paul Westerman. Therefore, while Ward Cohoon was alive, the ore could not be hauled directly to the new road south; Westerman's drivers had been forced to make a detour north first by way of Yellow Ford and Sombrero with the loss of mules and equipment and more than two days of time. Then Ward and Jonathan Cohoon had died, shot down on the same day, and with no one to stop them, the wagons had broken a new, short, and easy road directly to the east, which they were still using. This explained a great many things, including why Paul Westerman had been so eager to have him leave town. But it left one burning question still unanswered: had Westerman merely taken advantage of two murders, or had he caused them? *How long do I give him the benefit of the doubt? Cohoon thought grimly. How much doubt is there, anyway?*

The sound of a shot behind him made him look around quickly; three riders were coming over the ridge, separating as they approached. They were still much too far away for a rifle bullet to carry; the shot had been a signal. Cohoon looked ahead, and saw two riders detach themselves from the little caravan on the road, and spur toward him.

11

NAN MONTOYA lifted the brief, gaudy dress over her head, drew it whispering down about her, and came out of the smaller room, pausing in the doorway to look with some amusement at the young man who sat on the cot awaiting her. This was the second evening he had called to escort her to Miss Bessie's; he had been here during the day as well, but he still clearly was not resigned to finding her living in such a place. His expression made abundantly clear his opinion of dirt floors, mud walls, and the old woman crouching by the dead fireplace. He looked up quickly at Nan's appearance. She walked over and presented her back to him.

"You might as well make yourself useful, Lawrence," she said dryly, "after coming all this way to find me." When, uncomprehending, he did not move she said, "Button me, dearie."

There was always, nowadays, this compulsion that she could not resist, to make people accept her at her worst; it was easier, simpler, and in a sense more dignified to act out the part they expected of her now than to try desperately to crawl back into the ranks of the respectable, who would not have her anyway. The young man behind her began to fasten up her dress in a gingerly manner.

"We're not in Boston now, Lawrence," she said tartly.

"But, Nancy," he said, "you can't *like* it here. This hut . . . that place you work . . . that awful woman who runs it . . ."

"Miss Bessie's been kind to me," Nan said. "You should have seen the place where I was working in San Francisco when she hired me and gave me the money to come here."

"I did," Lawrence James said grimly. "And I understand your natural sense of gratitude and . . . and loyalty, but nevertheless you must see that this is no place for you. You belong—"

"Where?" she asked. "Where do I belong, Lawrence? At home? Is that what you're trying to tell me?"

"Nancy, I know that—"

"Two years ago," she said, and was still not able to keep her voice from trembling slightly at the memory, "two years ago, after Montoya died, I wrote home for help. I *wanted* to come home, then."

"I know," James said, fumbling with the tiny round buttons. "I know, but—"

"Do you know how long it takes a letter to travel from San Francisco to Boston? Do you know how long it takes the answer to get back? I was sick; I had no money; but I managed to live, counting the months. When the letter came . . . when it came, do you know what it contained, Lawrence?" She drew a long breath. "It contained one sheet of paper, and a line of handwriting. My father's handwriting. He asked me, if I had any decency left, not to hurt him or Mother further by communicating with them again or by using the family name."

James said, "I know. The Reverend Mr. Wyatt—"

"The Reverend Mr. Wyatt has no daughter," the girl said harshly. "She disobeyed his wishes and ceased to exist. That's what he wants, and that's what I want, Lawrence. From now on I'll make my own way, without asking anybody's help." She pulled away from him and walked into the other room, throwing aside the blanket that normally shielded the archway. She stopped in front of the mirror that hung on the far wall of the smaller room, and reached back with both hands for the remaining buttons of her dress. In the mirror she saw him come into the doorway and stop, not wishing to commit the impropriety of entering a lady's bedroom. "I'm sorry," she said quickly. "I'm sorry, Lawrence; I treated you badly, and it was sweet of you to come all this way to find me, but it would have been better if you hadn't. Don't you see I can't possibly go back?"

"As my wife?" he said. "Not even as my wife, Nancy?"

She swung around to face him. It was a moment before she spoke. "Do you mean that? Do you still want me—after what I did to you?"

The young man in the doorway drew a deep breath. "I love you," he said. "That makes it very easy to forgive—"

"Oh," she said, very softly.

"What is it?"

"Nothing," she said. "It's nothing, Lawrence. And it's very sweet of you to forgive me. Now, if you'd hand me that shawl on the bed, I think I'd better get over to the Double Eagle. It's getting late."

James did not move at once. "What is it, Nancy?" he asked again. "What did I say that was wrong?"

She smiled, coming forward. "I appreciate your forgiveness," she said, "but I don't think I want to live with it for the rest of my life. And it would be a mistake for us to get married, anyway. It would have been a mistake three years ago—even then my ideas used to shock you occasionally, didn't they, Lawrence?—and now it simply wouldn't work. I've seen a lot of things in the past three years, and I've learned a lot, too. It hasn't all been a loss, my dear. I have no intention of returning to Boston to sit in a corner with my hands demurely folded in my lap for the rest of my life. And that's what you'd expect, isn't it? In return for your forgiveness and all the trouble you've had in finding me again, I would in all fairness be obliged to make you a humble and decorous wife. Well, I can't make that bargain, because I wouldn't be able to keep it. So I think you'd better take the stage tomorrow alone. This is not the place for you, my dear, and I'm certainly not the woman for you. Goodbye, Lawrence."

She swept the shawl about her shoulders. Lawrence James turned without speaking and walked stiffly across the larger room to pick up his hat; at the door, he turned to look at her where she stood, by intent, framed in the archway in her dance-hall costume, waiting for him to go. When he spoke again, his voice was changed.

"Don't be a hypocrite in addition to everything else," he said, speaking in an odd, harsh way. "Why bother to try to spare me? Why not just tell me the truth: that you prefer the illicit company of a robber and jailbird to an honorable proposal of marriage?"

Startled, Nan said blankly, "What in the world do you . . . Oh!"

"Yes," James cried. "I mean your latest protector, the local badman who came to town with you; who shares this place with you. Do you think it's a secret? Do you think I haven't been told? But I was willing to overlook even that; after all, you seem to have a weakness for evil men, don't you, Nancy? First that scoundrel of a Montoya, with whom you ran away on the eve of our marriage, and now this outlaw, and how many in between—"

"Please go," Nan whispered.

"I thought there might be a spark of decency left," James shouted. "I thought that back in civilized surroundings, under proper supervision . . . but it seems you don't even realize your own position, Nancy."

"I'm sorry," she breathed. "I wish you hadn't . . . So it was revenge you wanted, after all?"

He was shocked out of his anger. "Revenge?"

"Yes. You didn't come here because you loved me, did you, Lawrence? You came all those thousands of miles because you hated me, because I made you ridiculous three years ago. So now you want to drag me home, all tarnished and bedraggled as I am in your eyes, and turn the joke on those who laughed at you. You want to look big and generous and forgiving at my expense. And what kind of a life did you have in mind for me, Lawrence? How often would I have been reminded of your kindness and my own unworthiness. . . . Go on, Lawrence. Don't say anything else. Just go."

"Oh, I'll go," he cried. "I'll leave you to your badman, if he ever comes back. He's been gone two days, hasn't he? He was warned to leave town. They're saying at the hotel that he won't be back; they're betting money on it. But you'll find somebody else, no doubt. . . ."

Then he was gone. She stood there long enough to let him reach the corner; then, driven by a sudden urgency she did not allow herself to analyze, she ran out, hurrying toward the Double Eagle, where somebody would know what Lawrence had been talking about.

12

THE CLEAR, accurate, and unsentimental voice met Cohoon as he came through the doors of the Dougle Eagle. He stopped just inside and stood watching Nan Montoya, by the piano at the end of the room, as she finished her ballad—enunciating the unladylike words of the refrain with a careful precision that left no doubt of their meaning. Cohoon moved to the bar during the loud applause that followed, and stood there while she sang a more innocent melody, in the same precise way. He turned to get his drink when she was through; turning again with the glass in his hand, he found her beside him.

She said, "The betting was five to three you wouldn't be back, Cohoon. You're costing a lot of people money."

He drained the glass and grinned at her. "Out where I was, ma'am, the odds were five to one."

She said, a little stiffly, "I have asked you to call me Nan. . . . Let's take that table in the corner before you explain that remark. I've been standing up all evening."

They walked across the room together. Once Cohoon paused briefly, as he saw Francis Paradine with several companions drinking at a table with a couple of Miss Bessie's girls. But the boy did not look up—if, indeed, he was sober enough to recognize faces—and Cohoon moved on to join Nan, who had signaled a barman to bring a bottle to the table. Seated, they regarded each other for a moment in an appraising way, as if years instead of days had passed since their last meeting.

She asked, "What did you mean about the odds being five to one where you were?"

"Why," he said, laughing, "there were that many fellows chasing after me."

"Westerman's men?"

He glanced at her quickly. "You keep your ears open, don't you, ma'am . . . I mean, Nan."

"They were saying here in town that Mr. Westerman had warned you to leave this part of the country. It seems he considers you responsible for the death of his son who died in the holdup for which you went to prison." Her glance touched the figure of the boy slumped drunkenly over the table in the center of the room; and her voice was sharper when she spoke again. "You went to prison for the Paradines; do you intend to die for them, too? Mr. Westerman has no real reason to hate you, does he? Instead of letting his men hunt you like a wild animal, why don't you just go to him and tell him who was really his son's partner in that holdup?"

Cohoon grinned, and shook his head. "That hand's been played," he said. "It's a little late to claim a misdeal now, even if it would help, which it wouldn't. I learned a few things while I was gone, Nan, among them that Westerman's motives aren't exactly what they seem—not that they ever were. He always did have the reputation of being a shifty kind of poker player."

She said, "Well, anyway, you got away." She studied him for a moment, and added, "You look mighty cheerful, for a man who's been riding for his life."

"Riding anywhere is a pleasure, after Yuma," he said. "And I was born on the Grant, remember; I'd deserve anything that happened to me if I let a handful of saloon hardcases catch me there. I took them straight across the Candelarias and back again; I reckon they're still trying to figure how I got that pony down a hundred-foot cliff." He shrugged his shoulders, and laughed, a bit embarrassed. "Reckon I sound kind of pleased with myself, for just getting away from a bunch of saddle bums who couldn't track a cow down a muddy road. It's just that . . . well, after being penned up behind bars long enough, a man starts to wonder whether he can still sit a horse or find his way across country the way he used to." He went on quickly, changing the subject: "You look as if our climate was agreeing with you. How are you getting along with Miss Bessie?"

"She's been very nice to me," Nan said, "and the customers seem to like me."

Cohoon said, "They should. I reckon you're something different from what they usually find in a place like this."

"Don't flatter me, Cohoon," she said. "The difference between one woman and the next isn't as much as some people would like you to think. . . . But you're right in a way, too. Do you know why they like me? I'm no prettier than some of the other girls in the room, and my voice is nothing remarkable, and my songs aren't really anything out of the ordinary. Do you know the real reason why they like hearing me sing?"

He shook his head. "Why?"

"Because I'm a lady," she said calmly. "Or was, and they can tell it, even in this getup. And it pleases their vanity to have a real lady singing bawdy songs to them. . . . Oh, I'm not feeling sorry for myself, Cohoon. I figured it out very carefully, eighteen months ago, when one of Montoya's friends found me starving and took pity on me and offered me a job in his place. I took stock then, and discovered that all I had to sell—besides what every woman has to sell, which seemed a poor way to make a living—was a passably trained voice and an air of refinement. The latter was a novelty in that part of San Francisco; I decided to cash in on it. I got one of my old evening gowns out of hock—a very demure and ladylike garment—and sang a hymn for my first number. They didn't know what to make of that, or of me either, in that place. I sang a couple more songs of the same order. I saw they were starting to get bored; the novelty was wearing off. So I cut loose with one of the songs Montoya used to sing when he'd had a few drinks, and they realized that I'd had a joke at their expense, and loved it. . . . After that, sometimes I'd tease them a whole evening with hymns and sentimental ballads before giving them what they really came to hear. It was very good for business, which I suppose is why Miss

60

Bessie hired me on her last trip to San Francisco." She smiled at him. "You don't approve, do you, Cohoon? I can see it in your face."

He said, "It's none of my business."

"No," she agreed, "it certainly isn't. But you'd feel better about it if I'd sing nothing but nice songs, wouldn't you? You'd feel better, but you wouldn't come back to listen tomorrow. It makes you feel uncomfortable to hear a well-brought-up young lady singing dirty songs to a lot of drunken men; it shocks your sense of propriety. But you'll come back tomorrow to be shocked all over again, don't deny it."

Cohoon laughed. "You're kind of hard on us men, aren't you, Nan?"

She said, softly and bitterly, "No, why should I be? I really owe a great deal to the two men in my life: My father, who insisted on my learning to sing in the choir, and Montoya, who left me a guitar and an inexhaustible supply of lewd ballads—fortunately I have a very good memory, even for words I don't quite understand. Between the two of them, I manage to make a living; in fact, I can even call myself moderately successful. The customers have been generous, and Miss Bessie is pleased enough that she's even willing to let me go back to choosing my own costumes, even if they don't display my ankles." She laughed briefly. "I can remember when the idea would have shocked me deeply, but now it seems a small indiscretion. But I feel I can put on a more effective performance in a less flamboyant garment."

Cohoon chuckled, regarding her critically. "Well, now you mention it, it's quite a dress; a man hardly knows where to look."

"That depends on the man," she said dryly. "Most of them seem to have no difficulty." After a moment she said with a quick smile, "I don't understand you, Cohoon, or perhaps I don't understand myself. You disapprove of the way I earn my living, you use me to help settle your private grudges, and still I seem to tell you a chapter of my life every time we meet."

"Why," he said with a drawl, "I take it as an honor, ma'am." Then he hesitated, and went on: "I forgot to mention, as I was riding out of town two days ago, a young fellow was asking for you at the hotel. I said nothing to him, figuring that if you'd wanted to be found, you'd have let him know where to look."

"That was good figuring," she said, a trifle grimly. "I wish some other people in this town had figured similarly. . . .

61

Well, I'd better get up and earn my keep. Are you staying?"

"I'll be here," he said.

She paused after rising, looking down at him. "I don't want to tell you your business, Cohoon, but Westerman's bound to learn of your presence in town. Hearing me sing isn't worth getting killed for, particularly when you don't care for my songs in the first place."

Cohoon grinned. "Thanks for the warning, but I doubt there's anything to worry about. Paul Westerman's playing his brand of poker and I'm playing mine. To have me get arrested for brawling the first day here was a good idea, but it didn't work. And if I'd just ridden out of town and disappeared, after being warned to leave, that would have been acceptable to most people, although there might have been a few questions asked. But a full-dress murder here in town . . . people wouldn't like that. They'd say that since it was a personal matter, Mr. Westerman ought to've done his own killing. And for all his gambling background, he's not the man to risk everything he's built here on the turn of a card—or his skill with a gun, either."

She moved her shoulders. "All right, if you want to wait, I'll be just long enough to sing a pretty song for you, and one not so pretty for the paying customers. Have a drink on the house to make it sound better."

He watched her move away among the tables, avoiding the reaching hand of a drunken man, and responding lightly to comments thrown her way. It disturbed him that she should seem more attractive to him tonight than ever before. It was improbable that she had changed markedly in two days; therefore it was his judgment that was at fault—a judgment that he had no reason to trust, in any case where women were concerned. Yet, as he watched her take her place beside the piano and begin to sing, he found himself toying with a notion that had first come to him when he looked at the blackened walls of the ranch house and told himself that it was just as well he was not bringing a bride home today, since there was no home left to which to bring her. He reached for the bottle and started to pour himself a drink, but changed his mind. It was not a decision to be made under the influence of liquor.

When she came back to the table, he rose to greet her. "Can you come outside for a few minutes?" he asked.

She studied his face briefly. "I suppose so," she said. "I'll tell Miss Bessie and get my shawl."

Outside, the night was clear and moonless, so that the

stars seemed brilliant and very close. The strong winds of the past few days had slackened temporarily; there was only a mild breeze, not enough to stir the dust. They walked down Creek Lane to the arroyo that cut it short, and a little ways down the edge of the arroyo to where the sound of the saloon and gambling places was a dim murmur behind them. The rest of the town was already quiet. Cohoon stopped and turned to look at his companion. Her face was a white oval in the darkness. She was the first to speak.

"I was worried about you, Cohoon. That's odd, isn't it, considering how short a time it is since we met?"

He said, "It's good to know. You were in my mind, too. Nan, I—"

He found it difficult to continue, under the steady regard of her eyes. It seemed suddenly a cold-blooded and unworthy thing he was about to propose; yet there was more than this behind his sudden silence. They faced each other for a moment without speaking. Then she stirred slightly; and suddenly she was in his arms. The kiss was warm and deeply satisfying—as satisfying as a kiss could be. At last she turned her face aside and stood for a moment, still in the circle of his arms, pressing her forehead hard against his shoulder. He could feel her trembling. She lifted her head abruptly.

"That," she said, "was probably a mistake, but I do not regret it."

"Nan—"

"No," she said. "We are both lonely people, Cohoon. Let's not pretend it was more than that."

She freed herself, and raised her hands to her hair. He watched her, and began to speak abruptly.

"I've been over at the Grant the past two days, as you know," he said. "The grass looks pretty good this year. It's thirty miles from road to road, and about the same from the river to the crest of the Candelarias. All that isn't fit for cattle, of course, but there's enough. I plan to build a cabin up by Willow Spring, handy to the new road, and hire as many hands as I can afford to round up what's left of the stock. I have a hunch Westerman's miners have been living high on Diamond C beef, but that kind's mostly too lazy to go after a cow that isn't standing out in plain sight, so there ought to be enough back in the breaks to make the start of a herd; and according to Van Houck, Father left enough to pay the taxes and carry me for a year or two."

He stopped as the girl before him made a movement as if

to speak, but she changed her mind. He could just make out the shape of her face in the darkness.

He said, "That much looks pretty good. Left alone, I ought to have the place in pretty good shape by fall—as far as living on it is concerned. It'll take a few years to show any kind of a profit, of course, after the way it's been left to run down. However, there're some other things you ought to know. Westerman's one of them; he claims to hate me because of Harry. Actually, I've learned he's got better reasons that concern his pocketbook. I figure I'm going to have trouble there. Also, somebody killed Father, and Jonathan, my brother, a couple of years ago; you may have heard of that. Maybe it was somebody just drifting through, although it doesn't seem likely, the way the thing was done. If it was, he's long gone, and I'm not going to waste more of my life chasing after him. But if it's somebody local. . . ." Cohoon shrugged. "I'm still not going to chase after him, although some people feel I ought to. I figure that sooner or later he'll come to me, not being able to stand the strain of having me around. When he makes his move, I'll have to move quicker, that's all. I don't figure he'll give me time to take it to the law, even if there was any law around here that would walk across the street to help me. . . ."

Nan was quite still; only her lips moved. "Cohoon, what are you trying to say?"

He drew a long breath. "I know. I'm going the long way around the barn, but I wanted you to know how things stood." He looked down into her face; after a moment, he laughed ruefully. "Father rode clear across the country when the time came for him to settle down. I never heard that he had any trouble asking the girl he picked out. Well, I reckon I'll never be the man he was in any respect."

"Are you asking me to marry you?" Her voice was gentle enough, but it held an edge of harshness.

"Yes," he said.

"Why?" she demanded.

He hesitated. "Do you want fancy words, Nan? Or do you want the truth."

"Try the truth," she said quietly.

"I've been five years in prison," he said. "I've got a big job to do out on the Grant, and I doubt I'll be able to do it alone."

She said, "I hear no mention of love."

He said, "I've heard all I want to hear of love; and I wouldn't be surprised but what you have, too. I will say this:

I need you, and I'll do my best to make you happy." After a moment, he said, "It's pretty soon for me to ask, I know. There's no need for you to answer tonight. I just got to thinking; this fellow from the East might be wanting to take you back with him. I thought I'd better let you know there's a place for you here, if you want it."

"I have a place here." She jerked her head toward the sound of music. "I don't *need* to marry anyone."

"I wasn't implying that you did."

She looked at him for a moment longer; then turned abruptly away, looking out toward the desert. "Is that really why you asked me tonight? Because of Lawrence James? Or was there another reason?"

Cohoon said, "I don't rightly know what you mean. The fact that you looked real pretty tonight, to a man just out of the hills, might have had something to do with it."

"I thought we weren't going to have any fancy words." Her voice was harder than it had been. "Tell me just one thing. Where did you stop in town tonight before you came to the Double Eagle? Who did you talk to?"

He frowned, puzzled. "You were the first person to whom I'd spoken in two days, Nan, except the bartender, to ask for whisky. I stopped nowhere else in town, since I'd had a bite to eat on the road about sundown."

She swung around to look at him. "You're telling the truth?"

"Yes. What—"

"Then you don't know? You haven't heard?" He did not speak, and she said, "We get the society news, even on our side of town. It has been publicly announced that Miss Claire Paradine is to be married next week, to your friend Westerman. But that would have nothing to do with your asking me, would it, Cohoon?"

He said quietly, "I didn't know."

"I . . . I'd hate to think you were again using me for revenge," she said. "A lifetime of revenge, Cohoon? You'd be the second man today who wanted me for that. Lawrence wanted to marry me to get even with me; to make me suffer for standing him up three years ago. Do you want to marry me to get even with her; to make her suffer?" He did not answer, and she said breathlessly, "Even if you did not know she had announced her wedding plans, you could still have been striking back at her—I think you were." She flung back her head to look at him. "The answer is no, Cohoon. No! If you want a reason, I'll give you the look on your face just now when you heard she was marrying Westerman.

65

You're still in love with her. And I don't want a man who's another woman's property; I've been through *that* once before!"

Then she was silent. After a second or two, Cohoon said, "It's your decision. I'll see you back now."

He reached for her arm, and she let him take it and guide her back along the arroyo bank to the end of Creek Lane. As they turned into the street, moving toward the lighted parts ahead, a figure stepped out from behind a nearby adobe shack, crying in a shrill voice:

"Get away from him, Nancy!"

Cohoon saw the gleam of the long-barreled revolver, and gave the girl a straight-armed push that sent her stumbling out of the line of fire. There was time for no more, as the gun discharged with a black-powder roar and a burst of flame that split the darkness apart for an instant and left it darker than before. Cohoon felt the sharp, club-like blow along the ribs; it threw him off balance. The gun fired again, thunderously close, and a third time; then, on one knee, he had the knife clear. The throw was good.

He got to his feet slowly. There was blood trickling down his side. Nan had picked herself up; he saw her run forward and go to her knees in the dust, heedless of her dance-hall finery.

"He'll be all right," Cohoon said, "unless his head's softer than I think."

He stepped forward and picked up the knife; that was the good thing about a knife, it gave you a choice of point or hilt. There were people running down the street now, drawn by the sound of gunfire; Nan would soon have help in caring for the unconscious man.

There was nothing for him here except a possible argument with the marshal; Cohoon started to walk on, but checked himself, looking down at the long-barreled revolver lying in the dust by Lawrence James's outflung hand. Even in the dark he could see that it was an old-fashioned cap-and-ball gun, converted to metallic cartridges; in its day it had been a fine weapon, elaborately engraved. The original owner's initials still showed on a gold plate set into the butt. Cohoon picked the weapon up and read the worn letters: *R. St.C. P.*

13

THE PARADINE HOUSE was dark except for the upstairs window of Mrs. Paradine who, Cohoon recalled, suffered from insomnia in addition to her other complaints. Cohoon walked up the steps and knocked on the front door. Presently light was brought along the hall inside, and the door was opened for him by a stout, dark-faced woman he did not know. Then Claire Paradine came down the hall, wearing a light-blue robe over her night-dress.

"I'll take care of this, Teresa," she said. "Just leave the lamp here." She waited until they were alone in the doorway before she spoke again. "Boyd, what do you want? You must be drunk to come pounding on our door at this hour."

He looked down at her. Her fair hair was loose about her shoulders and the lamplight was in it; she was an image out of the dreams that had kept his hope alive for five years. He realized that Nan Montoya had spoken only too accurately: she had been wise in refusing to accept, on any terms, a man who could never be more than partly hers.

He said, "I want to speak to your father, Claire."

"I doubt that Dad cares to speak to you, after the way you've behaved; and I think you show poor taste—"

He said, "Let's not discuss my shortcomings here. Will you get your father, Claire, or should I come in after him?"

"Boyd!" Then, shocked, she said, "Why, you're wounded! There's blood all down your shirt—"

"Never mind that," he said harshly. "Just get the Colonel down here. I have some property of his to return."

"But—"

There were footsteps behind her. "What's this?" Colonel Paradine's voice demanded. "What's going on here? Who—" He stopped a pace behind his daughter, clearly taken aback by the identity of the visitor; then he cleared his throat and spoke angrily: "Mr. Cohoon, I don't think I need to explain why you're no longer welcome here at any time, but particularly in the middle of the night. We don't keep Creek Lane hours here, young man!"

Cohoon said, "My errand won't take long, sir. I simply

came to give you back your gun. Next time you lend it, I suggest you pick someone who can shoot."

There was a moment of startled silence. Cohoon drew the long-barreled weapon from his waistband and held it out, butt-first.

"It is your gun, isn't it, Colonel? Your initials are on it."

"Where—"

"Does it matter where he tried to do the job?" Cohoon drew a long breath and said: "Colonel Paradine, a few days ago you gave me a sum of money in return for certain services. There's nothing to be gained by going into details; let's say only that it was not the payment I had expected. I should simply have refused the money, since I could never have brought myself to use it. Instead, I gave it to someone who had been kind to me." He was aware that Claire had moved slightly, but saw no reason to correct whatever impression she had drawn from his words. He continued to address himself to the Colonel in a formal way: "Sir, I admit that my action was ill-considered and unfortunate. Please believe that no conscious slight or insult was intended; and that I deeply regret any hurt my action may have caused any person in this household."

Neither of the two people facing him spoke; both were watching him with an air of bewilderment. Cohoon once more extended the revolver he was still holding.

"That ought to satisfy your honor, Colonel Paradine," he murmured. "Take your gun back now. Having received my apology, you should feel no need to find another lovesick boy to use it. Good evening, sir." He looked at Claire for a moment. "And my best wishes to you, ma'am. I hope you and Mr. Westerman will be very happy."

Then he was walking down the steps to the street again, with a giddy feeling due as much to anger as loss of blood. He strode away without looking back; presently he heard the door close behind him. A movement in the shadows made him swing around sharply.

"I've been looking for you, Cohoon," Bill Black said, coming forward.

"You've found me."

"Why did you run off, leaving an unconscious man lying in the street?"

"He was lucky to be unconscious. He'd have left me dead. Also, he was being cared for."

"I warned you when you first came back to behave yourself peaceably. The same evening, I also warned you to keep to the side of town reserved for people like you; and to stay away from the Paradines. . . ."

Cohoon said softly, "I said it once before and I'll say it again: a badge is a handy tool for a jealous man." The anger was loose in him, driving him on; it might as well be Bill Black as anybody. "You've done me a favor, Willie," he murmured. "I used to be ashamed of my brother's rough jokes, but no longer. He only made one mistake: when he dumped you into the river, he shouldn't have bothered to fish you out. But then he couldn't know what a sanctimonious hypocrite you'd turn out to be, skulking around a girl's house without nerve enough to—"

Black's voice was shrill. "You're under arrest, Cohoon!"

Cohoon laughed. "That's an easy way to get rid of your rivals. Tomorrow morning you can try arresting Westerman, and then the field will be clear."

"Unfasten your gun!" the marshal snapped. "Let it drop, carefully!"

Cohoon felt the grin grow thin and wolfish on his lips. "Why, certainly, Marshal," he murmured. He released the buckle without looking down, and let gun and belt fall. "The knife, too?" he asked gently, and saw Black's eyes widen as the other realized his error.

Then the marshal's hand was swinging down to his holstered gun; but the heavy knife was already lying in Cohoon's palm, and his arm was rising for the final snapping movement that would bury the weapon in the other's chest, just below the badge pinned to the white shirt. He knew a moment of regret; there was no sense to this. It was just the anger and bitterness inside him finding the nearest outlet. But it was too late to turn back, and he judged the distance and balanced the knife for the amount of spin that would place it point-first at the target. . . . There was a cry at his left, and a flash of movement; and he checked the throw at the last instant, as Claire Paradine threw herself between the two men.

"Boyd, Marshal—"

It was Black who spoke first, in a shaken voice. "Miss Paradine, this is no place for you. You might have been shot!"

She said tartly, "With a gunfight here in the street, I could just as easily have received a bullet inside the house. What's the meaning of this, anyway, Marshal Black?"

Cohoon said, "He's protecting you, Claire. I had been warned not to bother you again."

Black's flush was visible even in the darkness. "Ma'am, I just figure that the respectable people of the community have the right to be protected from the less desirable elements, at least in their own homes."

Claire looked from one to the other of the two men; suddenly she smiled, turning to the marshal. "Why, that's mighty sweet of you, Mr. Black," she said. "And I'm sure we appreciate your concern, and maybe Mr. Cohoon *is* a little out of place among respectable people, but you'll have to forgive him tonight. He just came to return something of Dad's, and we're very grateful for his thoughtfulness. . . . Why don't you come up to the house a minute, Mr. Black? I'm sure Dad would like to know how well you look after us."

She had the marshal by the arm and was leading him away; there was nothing for Black to do but release the butt of his gun and make a show of escorting her home. Cohoon stood watching them go, and so caught the odd, questioning glance she threw in his direction just before the door closed. Frowning, he sheathed the knife, gathered up the fallen gunbelt, and turned away. . . .

The big kitchen of the Van Houck house was a light and cheerful and friendly place when he reached it. Presently he was sitting, shirtless, on a stool with his arms raised.

"Not so tight, Aunt Marthe," he protested. "Give a man room to breathe."

"All the blood runs out of you, you'll stop breathing," said Marthe Van Houck, shaking her gray head at him. "Such foolishness, to walk around all night with a hole in your side big enough for a team and wagon. There! You can let your arms down now; and move over by the stove so you don't catch cold while Van Houck is bringing a clean shirt from the store."

Presently the old trader came in, closing the door behind him. Cohoon took the shirt from his hands, unfolded it, and put it on. Finished, he saw Van Houck regarding him curiously.

"Who was it, my boy?"

Cohoon shrugged, and regretted the gesture; the wound was shallow enough, but it was becoming stiff and painful. "A jealous fool with a borrowed gun," he said.

"Not the man for whom you're waiting, then?"

"I don't know," Cohoon said. "Not the man, to be sure. But the gun. . . ." He frowned, and took the cup of coffee Mrs. Van Houck gave him, and sipped it thoughtfully. "Uncle Van, what does Colonel Paradine have to do with Paul Westerman these days? There is a connection, isn't there?"

"There's the daughter, who's marrying the man." Van

Houck's voice was elaborately casual. "You'll have heard of that, of course."

"Yes," Cohoon said. "I heard."

"And the Colonel's been speculating in mining stocks, from what I've been told, on advice from Westerman. Sooner I'd take advice from the devil, myself; but maybe the Colonel trusts his future son-in-law."

Cohoon said, "Then if the Colonel were heavily involved in one particular mining operation, and saw his profits threatened. . . ."

Van Houck said, "I don't know what you're driving at, Boyd. However, I have no confidence in Roger Paradine. He would never have lasted in this territory if he had not brought with him a fortune in gold—and I have never understood why, with all that money, he chose to settle here, since he makes it plain that he does not like our country. It makes one wonder. . . . Well, it's bad manners to question any man's past. Nevertheless, my money stays in the bank in Tucson; and your father shared my views. But I would never turn my back on Roger Paradine, Boyd; no one ever knows what a weak man will do if pushed hard enough."

Cohoon said softly, "Father turned his back on someone. And I was shot at tonight with Colonel Paradine's gun."

The two men looked at each other for a space of time. The old trader was the first to break the silence. "Be careful, Boyd. It would not do to make a mistake."

Cohoon smiled briefly. "You were less in favor of caution when the man in question was Paul Westerman."

"Paul Westerman has no friends in this town; no one would mourn him, once he was safely dead. But the Colonel is popular among the decent people."

"I've no intention of shooting him, and you're a bloodthirsty old scoundrel," Cohoon said grinning. He rose. "Tell me, is old Judge Clark still alive? I need legal advice; and I'd prefer to get it from someone I could be sure was not in Paul Westerman's pay. . . ."

14

THE BUILDING was diagonally across the street from the hotel, about fifty yards down from Van Houck's old trading post. The lower floor was devoted to a feed and hardware store.

The windows above were shielded by drawn blinds. As Cohoon walked across Main Street in the slanting morning sunlight, he thought he saw one of the blinds move perceptibly. He found the door opening on the alley between the buildings, and took the stairs to the second floor. There were two doors. He chose the one toward the front of the building, and knocked. The door was promptly opened by Westerman himself.

"Come in, Boyd."

He looked pleasant and friendly and important; the gold watch chain of prosperity gleamed on his waistcoat. The office behind him was surprisingly sumptuous, considering the raw and ramshackle look of the building in which it was housed. Cohoon stepped forward and casually pushed the door aside as if to make more room for himself to pass; it would not swing back flush to the wall. He glanced at Westerman, who chuckled, and said:

"All right, Rudy."

A bearded man moved into sight, looking at Cohoon in a hostile way. There was a gun in his hand.

Westerman spoke again. "Put it away, Rudy. . . . You've met Jack Rudy, haven't you, Boyd?"

Cohoon said, "Well, we've come close."

"I have to take a few precautions," Westerman said. "A successful man makes many enemies. . . . All right, Jack. Wait in the other room."

The bearded man hesitated, then moved reluctantly away, disappearing through a door at the rear of the office. Cohoon moved forward. Westerman closed the door behind him, and walked past him to sit down behind the great mahogany desk by the windows—an impressive piece of furniture to find, shiny and unscarred, so far from civilization.

"Have a chair, Boyd," Westerman said. "I suppose you came to congratulate me on my forthcoming marriage."

"Well, it was in my mind," Cohoon admitted dryly, "among other things."

"No hard feelings, my boy?"

"For that?" Cohoon shook his head. "The choice was hers."

"Or her father's," Westerman said blandly.

"What do you mean by that?"

"Why, I find that a little money applied in the proper quarter will buy almost anything, Boyd. Not that the girl herself was reluctant to be bought. Very few women are, if the price is high enough."

Cohoon hesitated, and said softly, "I did not come here to quarrel with you about Claire Paradine."

"But I want to quarrel with you, my boy," the older man said with equal gentleness. "You seem to have a knack for interfering with the plans closest to my heart. Once there was my son, whom you led to his death—or did you? There are rumors, but people are always making up interesting stories, aren't they? Whatever the truth, you certainly interfered then, in one way or another; and now you're back, still interfering. You saw Judge Clark last night, so I have no doubt you've got some interesting plans for obstructing certain business operations of mine, but we'll get to that in due time. Right now I'm talking about my marriage. I'm an ambitious man, Boyd, and I've selected a wife suitable for the position I hope to attain. The fact that she's lovely, and not overly intelligent—certainly not as clever as she thinks herself—and that her family is respected and prominent in the territory, all help to make her the ideal choice. There are other reasons which I won't bother to go into, including the fact that I'm human and not too old to find her desirable. . . . Sit still, Boyd. The picture behind you masks an opening, behind which is Jack Rudy with his gun aimed at your head."

Cohoon looked deliberately around. The painting was a dramatic one with deep shadows, in the center of one of which metal gleamed faintly. He turned back to face Westerman, and grinned.

"If his marksmanship hasn't improved since I saw him out on the Grant, he'd do better to aim for the body. . . . Go on, Mr. Westerman."

"My campaign has been a careful one," Westerman said. "When you left here to go to prison I could not have dreamed of entering the Paradine household, let alone aspiring to the hand of the daughter of the house. In the past five years, however, since silver was discovered locally, Colonel Paradine has been involved in some unfortunate investments. It's a strange thing how much a man will spend on no more than a forlorn hope of getting rich—particularly if he's once had money, and has let most of it get away from him. I find it difficult to understand, myself. Personally I always make a point of knowing the exact percentages of the game I'm bucking. . . . But to return to the subject of my future wife. Stay away from her, Boyd. I will not have her making a spectacle of herself, running into the street in her nightclothes to save your life. She's mine, bought and paid for; she represents a considerable investment in time and money. I will not

73

stand for having the property lowered in value before I take delivery, my boy. I mean that." He smiled abruptly. "But enough of that. Now, what was it you really came to see me about?"

Cohoon did not speak at once. He had to tell himself firmly that Claire Paradine, and whatever bargain she had made for her own or her father's sake, was no longer any concern of his. He remembered Nan Montoya's voice saying: *You went to prison for the Paradines; do you intend to die for them, too?* Yet it seemed that love was a habit that was hard to break; and she had run out to stop the fight the night before—a fight that could have had but one ending for him, since even if he had won, he would have been guilty of killing an officer of the law. . . .

"I suppose," Westerman was saying, "your visit has something to do with what you discovered out on the Grant."

"That's right," Cohoon said.

"I'm sorry the question had to come up," Westerman said. "I was hoping I could persuade you to leave town before you learned of our little shortcut."

Cohoon said, "Mr. Westerman, did Father ever give you permission to haul ore across the Grant?"

Westerman laughed. "I could say yes, and how would you prove I was lying. . . . No, my boy, he refused quite bluntly. He seemed to have a prejudice against mining in general and me in particular. It seems he resented my behavior at your trial. I suppose I can hardly blame him, although personally I made an effort to distinguish between private matters, and matters of business. No, Boyd, you're on sound legal ground if you block our road, which is what I suppose you intend to do. We have no right on your property whatsoever; we'll have to go back to hauling over Yellow Ford and Sombrero."

Cohoon glanced at him sharply; he seemed quite resigned —almost happy—over the prospect. It was fairly evident that he had some trick up his sleeve, which was not entirely unexpected.

Cohoon said, "No, you won't, Mr. Westerman."

Westerman frowned. "What do you mean?"

Cohoon said, "Here's the paper I had Judge Clark draw up for me last night. Read it and see what you think." He started to rise, checked himself, and grinned. "Reckon you'd better come around here to get it; otherwise Rudy's apt to blow my head off."

Westerman spoke to the wall: "All right, Rudy. . . . Put it on the desk, Boyd."

Cohoon tossed the legal envelope on the shining surface, and seated himself again, watching Westerman pick it up and withdraw the contents. A strange expression crossed the older man's face as he began to read.

"An agreement," he murmured, "concerning a right-of-way. . . . But this is most reasonable, Boyd!" He sounded surprised and a little disappointed, as if some plan of his had been spoiled.

"I thought so," Cohoon said. "Judge Clark said I was crazy."

"I can see his point," Westerman said, still reading. "Even the payments you ask aren't excessive, considering the expense of hauling by the other route. . . . Although I shouldn't admit that, should I, since it puts me in a poor bargaining position?" He laid the paper carefully on the desk. "I don't understand this, my boy. I don't understand it at all. I expected a fight."

Cohoon said, "I know you did."

"Boyd, what are you trying to do, buy my friendship?"

"Your friendship is nothing to me, Mr. Westerman. I'm just trying to find out if you're a murderer."

"A murderer. . . . Oh!"

"Yes," Cohoon said. "Your wagons were rolling across the Grant before Father and Jonathan were even decently buried. I've learned that much. If you didn't commit the crime, you certainly took quick advantage of it."

"I'm a practical man, Boyd. Once they were dead, and no one left to stop us, there was no sense losing money by waiting. But I was not responsible for having them killed."

Cohoon said, "That's what remains to be seen. I'm clearing the decks, Mr. Westerman. As long as your teamsters leave my stock alone, and you make payments according to that contract, you can haul all the ore in the Candelarias through the Grant. I'm not blocking you; I'm not even costing you much money. So there's no further need for you to have me killed or driven out of the country, unless you've lied to me about your part in the murders. If your men come after me again, I'll have to figure that the reason is that you're afraid of me . . . afraid of what I might learn."

"Aren't you forgetting something? Aren't you forgetting Harry?"

Cohoon got to his feet. "I don't think you'll have me killed for Harry at this late date," he said. "And as for Claire, it was a childhood thing which we've both outgrown. You have no cause for jealousy; and I have no intention of seeing her again. There's only one motive you could have for wanting me dead—"

Westerman, too, had risen. "I'll never be afraid of you, Boyd. But you're a sensible young man. I like your attitude and I'll remember what you've said. There's enough trouble in the world without borrowing more, isn't there?"

As Cohoon came out of the alley between the buildings, he saw the southbound stage in front of the hotel, loading for departure. One of the passengers was a young man whose hat was perched precariously on top of a bulky bandage that covered his forehead almost to the bridge of the nose. Cohoon felt his own bandaged side wryly, and watched the stage pull away, before going on about his business.

15

COLONEL PARADINE set down his coffee cup, dried his pale mustache carefully on his napkin, and looked at his daughter over the breakfast table. He broke the silence.

"How is your mother this morning, my dear?"

"A little better," Claire said, "now that the wind has let up some. It makes her terribly nervous when it blows so hard."

"I know." If it wasn't the wind, it was the heat, and if it wasn't the heat, it was the dust and dirt of this dreadful, barren country to which he had condemned them all. Colonel Paradine knew the litany by heart; and he had a moment of impatient anger. How much punishment was the woman going to exact for a single mistake—if indeed it had been a mistake? He saw his daughter note his anger and disapprove; he composed his face, took notice of her costume, and said, "You're riding this morning?"

"I thought I would. It seemed like an opportunity to get a little fresh air free of sand for a change."

"Why don't you take Capitan? He hasn't been exercised for a week."

"That great brute?" Claire laughed. "Get Francis to exercise him, Dad. He likes a horse he can beat with a club; and it might get some of the liquor fumes out of his head."

She rose, and the Colonel got politely to his feet. The girl looked very handsome in her blue riding habit, he reflected; it seemed that she had gained in poise and assurance the past few days. Well, becoming engaged often did that to a girl. It was a pity this miserable country had offered her so little choice—not that she was doing badly, not at all—but back home she would have had her pick of a score of suitors. Or perhaps not. The war had not left the Paradines much, back there; certainly not enough to live in a manner befitting their station. If he could only make his family understand that; if he could only make them realize that he had throughout acted wholly in their behalf and with no thought of himself at all. . . .

Claire had paused by the door. She was speaking. "What did Boyd mean by what he said last night, Dad? Where did he get your gun? He was wounded. Surely you didn't—"

The Colonel brought himself back to the present, and said stiffly, "I gave my gun to no one, I assure you, my dear. I was not even aware that it had left the house."

Claire glanced upward in the direction of her brother's room. "I see. So it was young Master Paradine up to his sneaking tricks! I declare, Dad, you've simply got to talk to him. It's bad enough that he spends his nights on Creek Lane and comes home drunk at all hours, or not at all—that looks fine for the family and the bank, doesn't it? But to plot against the man to whom we owe—"

Colonel Paradine said quickly, "Claire, I consider that debt paid! If Cohoon chooses to throw my money to a dance-hall girl, that's his business."

"He apologized."

"He did not apologize for suspecting me of trying to have him killed in a cowardly and underhanded way!"

"Well, apparently somebody did try; and a Paradine at that!"

The Colonel looked at his daughter sharply. "You're taking a great interest in Boyd Cohoon this morning, after making a public show of yourself over him last night. If Paul should hear of it—"

Claire laughed shortly. "Paul will undoubtedly hear of it, trust the neighbors for that. But I seem to be . . . to be developing a conscience, Dad. I couldn't quite bring myself . . . Taking five years of a man's life under false pretenses is bad enough, without watching him be killed on my doorstep as well."

"Are you sure it's a conscience you're developing, my dear?" the Colonel asked. "Are you sure it isn't just curiosity?"

"What do you mean?"

"I have seen it before," her father said. "Every time a young girl gets engaged to be married, all the men she can't have suddenly begin to look very interesting to her, much more so than when she was free to take her pick of them."

Claire laughed. "You're being ridiculous, Dad," she said firmly. "I wouldn't marry Boyd Cohoon if he was the last man on earth. Let that hussy have him. But it was my doing that he went to prison, and I can't forget it. So you'd better tell Francis to curb that sick pride of his. If he tries any more tricks, I'll go to Paul and tell him the truth about what happened five years ago!"

She was gone before her father could open his mouth to protest. He stood where he was until he heard the front door close; then he picked up his coffee cup and started to drink absently, discovered the cup was empty, set it down, and walked quickly out of the room. In the library, the revolver with the three fired chambers still lay upon the desk, uncleaned, as he had put it down the night before. He regarded it for a moment, and turned to speak to the houseman who was passing.

"Go up to Mr. Francis's room, Fernando, and tell him I want to see him here at once."

"But Señor, he is not there. He is not home yet."

"Oh," said the Colonel, and after a moment, "very well, Fernando."

He seated himself at the desk, brought the proper equipment from a lower drawer, and began to clean the revolver, discovering that the night's neglect had already allowed the primer and powder residues to attack the bore. This saddened him: the weapon was an old companion. It had seen honorable service in the war—and his service in the war *had* been honorable, the Colonel reminded himself firmly, to the very end. Well, almost to the end. It was only when defeat and ruin had become bitter facts that had to be faced. . . .

"You wanted to see me, sir?"

He looked up, to see his son in the doorway. The boy's clothes looked as if he had slept in them. His hair was untidy, and his eyes had a puffy look. But his voice, as always, was cool and insolent.

"I met Fernando in the hall. He said—"

"Where have you been?"

"I spent the night with a friend, sir."

The Colonel said, "No doubt. You seem to have a great many hospitable friends these days, Francis, or is it always the same one? Never mind. Come here. Tell me, when was the last time you saw this gun?"

The boy moved forward, and stopped by the desk, finding

78

it necessary to steady himself against it. He looked at the revolver, and laughed aloud.

"So he brought it here. I should have guessed that he would, when I learned it was gone. Our Mr. Cohoon has a direct mind, doesn't he?"

"Francis, think carefully before you speak. Are you admitting that you took my gun and gave it to a—"

"Dad, stop sounding like a policeman." Francis regarded his parent across the desk. "I borrowed your gun, certainly. If that is a crime, sir, I apologize; but I'd got a little drunk the night before and lost mine in a card game. I needed a weapon to wear until I could win it back—which I did last night." He laughed. "So there I was, sitting with two guns in my belt, and this easterner came in asking for Boyd Cohoon in a blustering manner. He'd had some drinks up the street, and I guess they don't teach them to hold their liquor back there. Cohoon had taken that new girl outside. Somebody headed the fool in the right direction, just to see the fun. He was a poor-looking specimen; I doubt he'd had a fight since he was six years old; Cohoon could have held him off with a finger and blown him over with a breath. So, having a gun to spare, I slipped outside and passed it to him as he went by, to make things a little more interesting."

They faced each other for a long moment; it was the Colonel whose glance dropped away. There was a silence, during which Francis moved to a nearby chair and sat down, lying back and stretching out his legs gratefully.

"Don't lecture me on gratitude, Dad," he said presently. "I asked nothing of Boyd Cohoon, and owe him nothing. If you want to hand him money to spend on his pet songbird, that's up to you. If Claire wants to create a public scandal by using her charms to save him from arrest. . . ."

The Colonel licked his lips and said, "I'm not concerned with whether you like the man or not, Francis. I'm beginning to find him quite distasteful myself. But that's a different matter entirely from being a party to a treacherous attempt on his life. It reflects on the entire family—"

"Why?" the boy asked coolly. "What's a little more treachery to us, sir? Isn't our whole life—our position here—built on treachery? I'm surprised to hear *you* use the word, sir." He rose deliberately to his feet, while the Colonel sat pale and speechless. Half way to the door, he paused. "I'll admit that you have grounds to criticize my judgment; I should have given the easterner my own gun, which was unmarked. I apologize for the mistake." The boy regarded his father calmly. "For that alone. Nothing else. The only crime is being caught. Isn't that right, sir?" He turned away.

"Francis!"

The boy stopped. The Colonel rose slowly, leaning against the desk for support. "I've long wanted to talk to you about this, Francis, to explain—"

"Mother has explained it quite adequately, sir," Francis said. "She's quite bitter, of course; I have taken that into account. She feels that you betrayed a sacred cause. Personally, I have nothing but admiration for a man who can get away with a whole wagon-load of gold. There's only one question I've been wanting to ask, sir. You must have had some assistants; did you divide with them, or did you"— his glance touched the revolver on the desk—"or did you insure their silence by more permanent means?"

Colonel Paradine braced himself against the desk. He ignored the question that brought up ugly memories he had tried for twenty-odd years to erase from his mind.

"It wasn't anybody's gold, Francis," he said. "I want you to understand that. I was in command of the escort; we were to buy supplies; but long before we reached our destination there were no longer any supplies or troops to receive them. It would have done nobody any good but the Yankees. And there was nothing left at home, nothing. The war had been through there; your mother and the baby—that was before you were born—were living on the charity of friends. . . ."

The boy facing him smiled thinly. "Why, there's nothing to apologize for, Dad," he murmured. "We've lived off that money ever since, Mother and Claire and I, even after we learned where it came from. None of us have gone off to starve in honorable poverty, have we? That leaves us small room to criticize." He hesitated, and spoke in a different tone: "But as far as Boyd Cohoon is concerned, shouldn't we look at the matter practically? It seems to me that my little effort last night can be criticized only on the grounds that it failed."

"What do you mean?"

Francis said, "Well, aren't you pretty well involved in some of Paul Westerman's mining ventures, the Lucky Seven in particular? I suppose you know that Cohoon can cut the profits of that mine to a trickle by denying Paul passage across the Grant."

The Colonel was shaken. "What's this about the Grant? What has Cohoon to do with the Lucky Seven? It's several miles west of his boundary line, as I understand it."

Francis regarded his parent with youthful contempt. "You mean you put money into it without riding out to take a look? Or even glancing at a map?"

"Paul assured me—"

"He's assured a lot of people; that's the way he got rich. Why, it's a simple matter of geography, sir—" The boy went on to explain the situation. "So you see, Cohoon's got the Lucky Seven practically bottled up, if he wants to be stubborn like his dad. Of course Paul will fight, but fighting can be expensive. . . . Another thing; if my dear sister makes much more of a fool of herself over the man, Paul may decide to find himself a wife with a little more discretion, even if he doesn't start wondering just what's the tie-up between his future inlaws and this handsome ex-convict. And if Cohoon should ever chance to mention where he got the ten thousand dollars he bestowed on his dark-haired canary. . . . I understand the marshal paid us a visit last night, at Claire's urging. Did he happen to ask about the money?"

"Why, no. He just stayed a minute."

"Well, he'll be back, sir." Francis smiled unpleasantly. "He's been showing some interest in that money; he seems to think it may possibly have been part of the Lucky Seven payroll that was stolen. He's bound to turn up something pointing to this house. When he comes, are you going to tell him who gave Cohoon the money—and why?"

16

DINNER AT the Van Houcks' was a meal involving a large quantity of food and an extended period of time. There was pie for dessert.

"There!" Mrs. Van Houck said, sliding the last segment on to Cohoon's plate. "Now you will not neglect your old friends to go staying in hotels and eating in cafés where they boil everything in stale grease, *hein!* Now you know this is your home whenever you're in town, and don't wait for some man to shoot a hole in you to come here!"

Cohoon said, "Thanks, Aunt Marthe. I . . ." He hesitated, searching for the proper words.

"Ah, eat your pie and be quiet," said Mrs. Van Houck. "Too much talk at the table is bad for the digestion. I get more coffee."

Van Houck asked, "Did you have any success today?"

"I saw Westerman," Cohoon said. "The next move—if there's going to be one—is up to him."

"Your dad would turn over in his grave, to know you'd given permission for those wagons to cross the Grant."

Cohoon said, "Father was stubborn, and he loved to fight. I'm not stubborn, and I don't like to fight. I've got two jobs, Uncle Van: to get the ranch back on its feet, and to find a murderer—in that order of importance. I'm not going to take on a quarrel with Paul Westerman about where he runs his wagons as well. There's only one man I want a fight with, the man who shot down Father and Jonathan; and if I could turn him over to the law without a fight, I'd do that. As far as Westerman's concerned, he started hating me because of a mistaken belief, for which I was responsible. There's more between us now, maybe, but I can't forget that the initial fault was mine, and make some allowances." He grimaced wryly. "Besides, the ranch can use the money Westerman's going to pay for the privilege of continuing to use that road. I've made one big, expensive gesture for my pride's sake since I got back; I can't afford another."

Van Houck was silent, possibly fitting these words into the pattern of what he already knew and guessed. There had never been any open discussion of the past between them. He asked no questions about it. Presently he said, "How did you make out hiring riders to work for you?"

"I got a couple of hands lined up," Cohoon said. "All of our old crew seems to've drifted away, though."

"They were encouraged to drift," Van Houck said. "At least, they couldn't seem to stay out of trouble with Jack Rudy, Westerman's *segundo*, and his gang of hardcases. It could be that somebody was afraid they might have seen too much, the day of the murder. They were first to pick up the trail, remember?"

Cohoon glanced at the older man sharply. "Uncle Van, you just keep pointing me at Westerman and shoving like hell. What's the matter, is his new store causing you trouble?"

The old trader said, "Ah, perhaps I am prejudiced, my boy. To me, the man is a crooked tinhorn gambler with a holdout ace and a nasty little derringer up his sleeve. . . . But let's not fight about Paul Westerman." He hesitated, and went on in a slightly different tone. "Come into the other room, Boyd. I have all the papers on your dad's affairs and what I've done with them since his death."

Cohoon glanced at the windows, and said, "They'll keep.

It's dark, and I'd better be on my way; I'd like to get out of town without leading a parade, for a change."

"But—"

Rising, Cohoon clapped Van Houck on the shoulder. "Uncle Van, I don't need to see any papers."

"You need to see these." The older man's voice had changed still more, so that Cohoon looked down at him quickly. "You will have to look at them carefully, Boyd, and then you must decide if you should have me put in jail. . . ." He checked himself quickly, as his wife came back into the room with two cups of coffee, which she held out to them, laughing.

"Take them into the living room, so I don't fall over you while I clean up in here."

Her husband and Cohoon obediently carried the cups into the other room. Van Houck lowered himself into a deep leather chair, and looked up at Cohoon with misery in his eyes. There was a lengthy silence.

"Marthe doesn't know," the old man said at last. "It was . . . it was Westerman, and his new store, and his low prices. He loses money on everything he sells, Boyd; I know, because I have tried to meet the prices and it is not possible. He is trying to drive me out of business—me, Van Houck, who was here before there was even a town on this spot! I once said *I* had money in the bank in Tucson. That was a lie; it is all gone. So . . . so I borrowed from the other account, your dad's account. . . ."

After a moment, Cohoon said, "Why would Westerman want to drive you out of town, Uncle Van?" The older man did not speak, and Cohoon went on: "Would it have anything to do with the Grant?"

"Well—" Van Houck hesitated. "Well, he did come in and talk to me after your dad's death, in the smooth and slippery way he has—"

"About what?"

"About . . . about forgetting to pay the taxes, so that . . . so that the property would come up for sale. . . . I didn't do it, Boyd. The receipts are on the desk; you can see them for yourself, all in order. I wouldn't—"

"I know," Cohoon said gently. "And it was after that the new store went up?" The old man nodded unhappily. "Is there any money left?" Cohoon asked.

"Why, yes," Van Houck said. "There is what I told you. But there was a great deal more, as the papers will show—"

"To hell with the papers," Cohoon said. "What are you

getting all upset about, Uncle Van? You've lent money to us more than once; now you've borrowed some. I'll take out my interest in Aunt Marthe's apple pie. It you want to make it look legal in case something should happen to me, draw up some kind of a paper and I'll sign it next time I'm in town." He found his hat, and started for the door, and looked back at the old man still sitting there. "Damn it, Uncle Van," he said angrily, "I've got few enough friends left; I can't afford to lose one because of a bit of money. Clean out the whole damn account if you like, but stop looking at me like I was an Apache on the war path."

"Boyd, I—"

Cohoon said, "I'll see you in a couple of days. Tell Aunt Marthe good-by for me."

He picked up the bedroll he had set by the door earlier, threw it over his shoulder, and left the house. Outside it was dark. The Van Houcks' place was near the edge of town, which, blocked here by the same arroyo that cut Creek Lane farther west, had not grown much in this direction. As he lashed the bedroll behind his saddle, Cohoon could look out over the desert to the north and east. A sliver of a new moon hung in the sky near the horizon, enlarged to unreal proportions by some trick of the desert air. He mounted, and headed past the outlying buildings in that direction, meaning to circle the town in preference to riding through it and having his departure noted.

After a moment he glanced back and saw the light in Van Houck's living room, where the old man was doubtless still sitting, staring miserably at the wall. Reflecting on this situation, somewhat grimly, he did not pay much attention to his surroundings, so that when a small boy darted out of the shadow of a nearby shack, and the horse shied, he was almost unseated. It took him a second or two to bring the animal under control.

"Watch where you're running, kid!" he snapped at the child, who was watching with bright-eyed interest this activity for which he was responsible.

"That's a no-good horse, *si?*" the boy said. "My uncle, he sell you a better one. You are the señor Cohoon?"

"I am the señor Cohoon."

"Nan wants you at the Double Eagle. Come to the side door. At once, *muy pronto.*"

As he had come, the kid darted away. Cohoon started to shout a question after him, but thought better of it. He hesitated a moment, then sighed and swung the horse around. A warning instinct caused him to follow the outskirts of town westward, rather than head directly for his destination; enough questionable things had happened during the past few days to make it seem unwise to ride blindly into a dark alley on the word of a small, unidentified boy.

At the point where Creek Lane found its end against the arroyo, Cohoon dismounted, and tied the horse by the adobe shack from behind which, the previous evening, the wild-eyed youth from the east had opened fire with Colonel Paradine's revolver. The memory made caution seem even more advisable. A dirty alley ran behind the palaces of pleasure on the east side of Creek Lane. Cohoon moved down it deliberately, gradually engulfed by darkness, and the sound of music, laughter, and loud voices from the surrounding buildings, that made his hearing useless. At the rear of the saloon adjoining the Double Eagle, Flagler's place, he paused to look the neighborhood over as far as the scant light allowed.

The space between the two buildings was less than ten feet, and totally unilluminated except by a narrow strip of night sky. He could barely make out the shape of the dance-hall's side door. A dozen men could be standing in the darkness on either side, totally invisible. It they weren't, Cohoon reflected, he was certainly wasting a lot of time. He felt the gun at his left hip, loosening it in the holster, but the dark was no place for firearms and there would be women in the buildings on both sides, neither of which looked as if it had been constructed stoutly enough to stop a stray bullet. He reached back for the knife, therefore, crouched, and threw himself past the corner at a run, sprinting for the dimly visible doorway ahead. If you were going to act like a suspicious damn fool, there was no sense making a halfway job of it.

The sound of merriment from the two buildings drowned the sound of his running. He reached the door without incident, paused briefly to look around—and to listen as much as the noise would permit. Then he turned and grasped the knob.

"Nan," he said softly. The door was locked.

This was warning enough. He was dropping even as a club or gunbutt swung for his head out of the darkness to the left.

"Here he is!" It was half a whisper, half a cry. "I told you he wouldn't come from the street. . . . Ah!"

The whisper ended in a gasp as Cohoon reached up with the knife; the movement was a savage and instinctive reaction to the blow that had barely missed his skull, and to the deceit and treachery that seemed to fill the night like a poisonous mist. First Van Houck and now this, he thought savagely as he struck; then his knuckles were warm and wet and it was too late for mercy and forbearance. It seemed to him that he had been waiting for this moment a long time—ever since he refused a fight with Jack Rudy, not knowing the name then, three days ago.

A man could stay peaceful only so long; a man could take only so many betrayals. He was thinking of the previous evening, of Nan Montoya kneeling, full of pity and concern, in the dust beside the man who had tried to kill him. There had been no pity for him, Boyd Cohoon, or concern for *his* wound. He should have known then what to expect.

There were men stirring at the street end of the narrow space, where the trap had been set. There was no one behind him and he could have fled, but the prison-bred hate was loose in him now, and he called softly:

"This way, boys. This way. Come and get it!"

They came. He never learned how many—too many for their own good. He marked one more, deeply and fatally, as they stumbled past searching for him; they turned at the bubbling cry and rushed in to overwhelm him. It was clear that they had little notion of how to deal with a knifeman in the dark, although by their accents there were some who should have known—south of the border, as well as among the Indians, the knife was an honored and respected weapon. But they came in fast, all together, to crush him to the ground; and he let them take him down and worked silently among them. Sixty seconds of panting murderous confusion followed; then the tight knot of men burst apart in sudden panic. A gun fired aimlessly. Somebody swore.

"Watch that shooting! Get a lantern! Don't let him get away!"

Another man said in a sick voice, "For the love of God, *amigos*, help. . . ."

"Here he is!" There was a sharp scuffle ending in blasphemy as the two men who had been fighting discovered each other's identity, one crying shrilly, "Well, what the hell do you expect, sneaking behind a man's back like a damn Indian!"

Cohoon, working toward the street covered by the deeper darkness along the wall, smiled wickedly to himself; they could well continue fighting each other back there for minutes longer. Then a door slammed noisily, and the flickering yellow light of a lantern showed on the street ahead, as someone came out of Flagler's place to investigate the disturbance—presumably a stranger in town, since the local population was noted for minding its own business.

Cohoon stopped moving and crouched low, waiting for the moment of inevitable discovery, when he would be silhouetted against the light, a fair target for the guns behind him. The others had become silent, recognizing the approaching opportunity. Cohoon felt the ground about him for a suitable missile but touched nothing but dust and hardback clay. He reached for the revolver at his hip and found an empty holster; the weapon had fallen out during the fight. The inquisitive stranger, swaying slightly, stepped into the mouth of the alley, holding the lantern high. He spoke in a thick and foreign voice.

"I shay, you chapsh, whatever sheemsh to be the trouble?"

Cohoon rose and hurled the knife; he was running as it left his hand, weaving from side to side. The lantern smashed; the light flared brightly and died away. A gun fired twice behind him, and a voice that he had heard before, somewhere, cried;

"That's enough! That's enough! Hold your fire!"

The stranger stepped into Cohoon's path, obeying the natural instinct to intercept whatever is fleeing. Cohoon drove a shoulder into the man, and let the impact throw them both to the ground. Despite the authoritative voice, there was still shooting behind him; splinters flew from the wall of the Double Eagle as he rolled; then he was picking himself up around the corner, momentarily safe. The front door was only a few yards away; he stepped through it.

Inside, Nan Montoya was singing. Her voice broke at his appearance; the song stopped. He turned and snatched up a rifle from among the half-dozen in the rack by the door. The gun was loaded. Cohoon cocked it and stepped back several paces, covering the door.

A man at a table cried, "Hey, that's my . . ."

His voice trailed away. Cohoon did not look aside. Running footsteps passed along the street, but no one entered. Presently Cohoon lowered the hammer of the borrowed rifle, and set the weapon back where he had found it.

"I thank you for the loan," he said courteously to the man who had spoken.

Then he walked the length of the room to Nan Montoya, still standing on the small stage. She was wearing a quite respectable and becoming evening gown tonight, he noted, instead of the bright and scanty dress of previous nights. She looked tall and quite lovely. He caught her by the arm and pulled her off the stage, marching her toward a door that he knew led to a room behind the stage. Half way there, he stopped, seeing Miss Bessie reach out a hand to take from the bartender a double-barreled shotgun sawed off at a convenient length. Cohoon spoke.

"I will not harm her," he said.

Miss Bessie looked at him for a moment, and lowered the stubby weapon to let him pass.

17

COHOON SHOVED the girl ahead of him into the small room, which was poorly lighted by one smoking lamp on the wall. The furniture consisted of some chairs, a table, and a couple of decks of cards. He kicked the door closed behind him. Nan turned to face him. Her dress had become somewhat disarranged by his rough handling of her, but she made no move to smooth it into place. She merely looked at him.

"Well, Cohoon?"

He spoke in an even voice. "About ten minutes ago, a Mexican kid stopped me as I was riding out of town. He had a message. Nan wants you, he said, come to the side door, *muy pronto*. I came. The door was locked. There were half a dozen men waiting, maybe more. It was hard to tell in the dark. There are fewer now than there were."

"I see," she whispered. Her mouth had a look of pain; perhaps anger also. "And you think I—"

He said, "I made no accusation. That's my story. What's yours, Nan?"

"I have no story," she said quietly. "I know nothing about it."

He studied her face, and found himself still liking what he saw—as he had from the first, on the trip north. There were judgments a man had to make on no better evidence than that. He made one now, even as the cynical part of his mind recalled that a similar judgment in the past had led to results that could fairly be called disastrous. On the record, he did not qualify as the world's best judge of character, particularly feminine character.

Nevertheless, he let the savage tautness flow out of him in a long breath. "All right," he said wearily. "I believe you."

"That's very kind of you," Nan said. "It's a pity you didn't believe in me a little earlier, before you squeezed my arm black and blue." She rubbed the bruised place and, the crisis being past, permitted herself to bring her hair and dress into better order. "You look like a herd of buffalo had run over you," she said without emotion. "Are you hurt?"

"No."

Her reply held sarcasm and some anger, not necessarily directed at him: "Six or eight men tackle him in a dark alley and he emerges unscathed! Well, I always heard you Westerners were a durable lot."

Cohoon said, "They were too many for the job. They got in each other's way. Father always said that the best way to deal with a gang like that, particularly in the dark, was to get them all on top of you and start cutting; they'd tire of the sport soon enough. They did."

Nan looked at him; a shiver seemed to go through her briefly. Then she shook her head and said, "Well, it's a pity your shirt isn't as tough as you are."

He grinned abruptly. "Every time I come around you, Nan, it costs me my shirt, one way or another. Last night—"

Her expression softened. "I wanted to thank you for that, Cohoon. For sparing his life. You had every right to kill him, the way he tried to murder you, but . . . Well, he did travel a long way to find me, whatever his motives, and I would have hated to see him come to harm." She watched Cohoon divest himself of the remnants of the shirt, most of which hung in rags about his waist. Her eyes noted the empty sheath and holster. "A shirt isn't the only thing you lost, apparently."

He grimaced. "I must have dropped the gun in the scuffle. Like Father used to say, the man who leans too heavily on firearms is apt to take an awful tumble some day. The damn things are never around when you need them. Then some fool came out of the place next door with a lantern. I had nothing to shoot and nothing to throw but the knife. I'll look for it on my way out—"

She said sharply, "You'll look for nothing more in that alley tonight, my friend. . . . What's that bandage? Did Lawrence actually hit you yesterday?" She read the answer in his face, and said angrily, "And I suppose you strode away, dripping blood, just to show how tough you are! Why didn't you say something?"

He said dryly, "You seem concerned with the fellow on the ground, ma'am."

"He was hurt. You didn't seem to be; why shouldn't I . . . Ah, what's the use? Anyway, you seem to've started it bleeding again. Sit down while I fetch some water and bandages, and a shirt if I can find one." She turned away from him, bent over, and her skirts made a whispering sound; then she was turning back, smoothing down her dress again. "Here. In case you have visitors."

He looked at the little nickel-plated five-shot revolver that had been put into his hand. The girl was already at the door when he spoke.

"Nan."

She stopped. "Yes?"

"I'm sorry."

"No need to be," she said coolly. After a moment she went on, "Assuming I had no hand in it, Cohoon, who used my name?"

"I don't know," he said. "I heard a voice—a man's voice—that seemed familiar, but I couldn't place it. I don't even rightly know what they were after."

"Why, to kill you, of course!"

"One man with a rifle could have accomplished that as I was leaving Van Houck's a lot more efficiently than a gang with fists and clubs."

She moved her shoulders briefly. "It sounds to me as if you were just looking for complications. Lock the door after me."

Then he was alone, listening to the steady beat of the piano and the muffled sounds of gaiety filtering back from the front of the building. A considerable interval passed before he heard her footsteps returning. He crossed the room to let her in. She went past him, and deposited her burden on the table; turning, she tossed him his hat, somewhat battered and dusty, and held out his gun. "That's all I could find out there; that, and a broken lantern, and some bloodstains. Quite a few bloodstains. I don't think I'll ever trap you in a dark alleyway, Cohoon."

He grinned. "From you, it would be a pleasure, ma'am. Well, somebody got themselves a good knife; Father made it himself out of an old file. Took him a couple of weeks to get it balanced right, I remember him telling me."

She was tearing strips from an old bedsheet. "Your dad was quite a man, wasn't he, Cohoon?"

"More man than I'll ever be," Cohoon said. "I always was the runt of the family—the white sheep of the family, Jonathan and Stuart used to call me. I reckon none of them would think much of the way I was handling things."

She said, "I suppose they'd have torn Mr. Westerman into little pieces by this time, wouldn't they? And the Paradines—

what would your father and brothers have done to the Paradines, Cohoon?"

He glanced at her quickly. "What do you mean?"

She laughed. "Sit down over here by the light and let me fix you up. . . . Why, it occurred to me last night to wonder where Lawrence could have got a gun. I know he never owned one back home—or even fired one, to the best of my knowledge—and while he could have bought one for the trip, it seemed unlike him. So I asked some of the girls, and learned that just after Lawrence marched out of the place telling everybody what he was going to do to you, young Paradine slipped outside. He was carrying two guns when he left, and only one when he returned."

Cohoon said, "So that's it!"

"Have I told you something you didn't know? You were quick enough to pick up the gun before anyone could see it; that was one of the things that started me thinking. It was obvious that you'd recognized the weapon."

"You're a clever girl, Nan."

"Am I?" She put her hands on his shoulders and turned him to a convenient angle. "Sit still now. Your friends seem to have an odd way of expressing gratitude."

Cohoon said, "I don't suppose Francis Paradine feels much gratitude toward me."

"You saved him from prison, didn't you?"

"Not for his sake. As far as Francis himself was concerned, he could have hanged for all of me. I suspect he knows that; probably he resents it."

"I can see why your family might have thought you a little peculiar, Cohoon," Nan said dryly. "Every time somebody tries to kill you, you always manage to figure out a good excuse for them. . . . There's something else I've heard, just keeping my ears open, that I don't know if I should tell you. This trader, Van Houck, the one with the long beard, how much of a friend of yours is he?"

"What have you heard?"

She said, "It was rumored around town that he was almost broke about the time your dad and brother were shot. Afterwards, his store seemed to take a new lease on life. He handled the estate, didn't he?"

"I wouldn't spread rumors like that," Cohoon said.

"I'm not spreading them," Nan said, working deftly with the scissors. "I'm just telling *you* what I've heard, since the matter concerns you."

"It isn't wise to hear too much, Nan," he said gently.

She raised her head and laughed in a spontaneous way. "Why, the man's threatening me! And I was merely trying to be helpful."

"Not threatening," Cohoon said. "Just warning. There were Mexicans in the bunch that tackled me outside; and I even thought I heard some words that sounded like Apache."

"What are you driving at, Cohoon?"

"Why," he said, "Paul Westerman seems to hire only American riders. And there's only one other man I can think of who could conveniently muster enough men for a trap like the one I ran into tonight, and expect them to keep their mouths shut afterwards."

"Who do you mean?"

"This outlaw called the General," Cohoon said. "The one who raided Westerman's mine office a couple of days ago."

"The General! But why should—"

"I wish I knew," Cohoon said wryly. "But who else could have set up the deadfall, and cleaned up so tidily afterwards? Willie Black said he had agents in town; in fact, the whole town's mighty upset about whoever's feeding the General his information. Willie seemed to think I might have had a hand in lining up that last job for him." He grimaced. "So I have the law on my neck with that notion, and the General himself for some unknown reason, if it was his outfit. I've never even met the man—"

"How do you know?"

He looked at her quickly. It was his turn to ask, "What do you mean?"

"The story is he's a Mexican revolutionary who crossed the border to save his skin. But it's just a story," Nan said quietly. "I've heard a lot about him since I came here—everybody talks about him, particularly since the robbery here in town—but I've still not heard of anybody who knew him down in Mexico. Nor have I met anybody who admits to having seen his face."

After a moment, Cohoon grinned. "I say it again: you're a clever girl, Nan."

"It's easy enough to put on a mask and a fancy uniform," she said. "So, how do you know you haven't met him? And all this business about the man here in town who gets information for him—for all we know, the General himself lives here in town, gets his own information, and sends a message to his men out in the *malpais* when he needs them. He slips on his conspicuous uniform, joins his gang for the job, leaves them when it's done—maybe he even joins the posse afterwards and helps chase them." She moved her shoulders. "For all you know, Cohoon, the General may have a perfectly good reason to want you dead. Why, he may be practically a friend of the family."

Cohoon said quickly, "Van Houck's too old to ride—"

Nan said, "Van Houck's too old, young Paradine's too drunk, his dad's too respectable, and Westerman hires nothing but American riders. And then there's the marshal, with his air of righteousness, the son of a man who's supposed to've got rich through robbery and murder; maybe it runs in the family." She shrugged. "*Somebody* robbed the Lucky Seven office. And *I* don't think it was a Mexican bandit."

"Would Westerman rob himself?"

"Why not? It wouldn't cost him anything; he'd just be shifting the money from one hand to the other." She laughed. "Cohoon, don't push me into a corner. I'm just telling you what I've been thinking. Maybe it's all wrong; I'm just a poor girl from the east without much experience with violence and lawlessness. . . ."

He said, "I hope you haven't told anybody else about your thoughts."

She shook her head quickly. "I've a well-developed instinct for self-preservation, my friend. I keep my mouth shut, except with people I trust . . . even if they don't trust me," she added teasingly.

"I said I was sorry."

Her smile faded. "There's no reason for you to trust me, none at all. In fact, any man who trusts a girl in a place like this is a fool." Her voice was bitter. She went on without looking up, "Lift your arms now, so I can get this off. . . . A woman bandaged you, didn't she? That's right, I did hear you went straight to the Paradine house afterwards. To return the gun before it led to embarrassing questions, no doubt. I will say this for you, Cohoon, you're a persistent sort of a man. Once you stick your neck out for somebody, you just keep it stuck way out, don't you?" Cohoon did not speak, and Nan went on as she worked: "I'll have to give her credit; she patched you up very neatly. I'd have said she was the type to faint at the sight of blood."

"You misjudge Claire Paradine," Cohoon said, deliberately provoking. "She can probably ride better and shoot straighter than you."

"That shouldn't be hard," Nan said, "since I've never had a horse off a bridlepath, nor fired a gun, in my life. That pistol I lent you is one Montoya liked to wear in his boot.

93

In an emergency I could probably make a noise with it, but that's all. But if I'd lived out here all my life, like she has, I'd certainly expect to be able to . . ." She glanced up, suddenly suspicious, and swift color flooded her face. "You're teasing me, Cohoon."

He nodded, smiling. "The bandage was made by Mrs. Van Houck. Nan, you're jealous."

"Yes," she said.

He looked down at her. Blushing, she was quite beautiful, and he said, "Then this seems a good time to repeat the question I asked you yesterday."

"The question . . . Oh!" She hesitated, and he found the suspense more difficult to bear than he had expected; then she shook her head. "The answer's still the same," she said, and looked up at him. "Even if . . . even if there weren't other reasons against it, you'd never be able to forget where you found me."

"I found you on a stagecoach going north," he said. "Anyway, that's the past. Forty years from now, we'll be remembering it fondly. We'll be telling the young ones of the good old days when grandpa spent five years in Yuma and grandma sang in a honky-tonk—" He saw the little smile that she could not restrain, and added quickly, "I would do my best to make you happy."

The smile died. "I don't doubt it," she said. "But your best isn't good enough. You would always be hers and not mine. I . . . I have one worthless wedding ring, Cohoon. I can do without another."

He glanced at her quickly. "Montoya? Is that the way it was?"

She said, "I did not intend to tell you. After all, it's not much better to have been deceived than to have been deliberately wicked. But, yes, I ran away and married him, against my family's advice. Advice?" she laughed. "I was forbidden to see or speak to him, even to say good-by. I was told that I was to marry Lawrence—a good match. So, I ran away. We were married on the ship. He was a very charming person, Raoul Montoya, even when he was drunk, which was often. Of course, he loved to shock me—educate me, he called it. I was very easily shocked in those days. I think, if I were given it to do over, I would act the same. He was a better man than Lawrence, at any rate. He made his living at cards —and his death as well; he was killed one night in San Francisco, about a year later, over the question of where he had found a third king to complete a full house. I think that's correct. I never got those poker terms quite straight in my mind. . . . Please keep your arms up so I can finish this job."

Cohoon said, "This is none of my business, Nan. I did not mean to pry."

She said, "You might as well know; and I'll always remember that you asked me to marry you before you knew. . . . Of course, cards were considered an invention of the devil at home, and anyone who as much as touched them lost all hope of salvation. . . . Well," she said with sudden briskness, straightening up, "that ought to hold you together until somebody shoots another hole in you. I'll save the rest of the sheet. You'll undoubtedly be needing it before long. . . . Oh, about the wedding ring. Well, after Raoul was dead it turned out that he already had one wife when he married me. She came around to claim his belongings, not that there was a great deal to claim. The guitar and gun were in a pawnshop; I got them back later. I suppose they're legally hers, too, just as he was." She looked at Cohoon directly. "So from now on I'm making sure I have clear title to the property before I buy, Cohoon, and you don't qualify."

He heard her through, and rose, pulling the fresh shirt over his head and tucking it in. He reached for his hat. "Your pistol's on the table," he said. "I thank you for the help."

"Don't act offended; you'll remind me of Lawrence," she said, smiling. "Where are you going now, to the ranch? Or perhaps you'd better not tell me; then, if someone attacks you on the way, it won't be my doing."

He said deliberately, "I'll probably make dry camp tonight between here and Black's Ferry—I suppose people still call it that in spite of the new bridge. Tomorrow I'll head for Willow Spring and see how things look at the east end of the Grant; then I'll have to pick up the pack I cached the other day when Westerman's riders came after me, and track down the mule I turned loose. After that I'll see about building some kind of shelter and finding out how much stock I've got hiding out back in the foothills. I want to get some notion of what's to be done before I start paying out wages to a bunch of riders." He looked at her for a moment. "If you should need me, send a messenger to Willow Spring."

"You'd come, after tonight?" She laughed softly. "You're a fool, Cohoon. And I will not need you. There'll be no messenger from me. That's definite, so you can govern yourself accordingly." She walked to the door with him. "But it was nice of you to make the offer. And I'll remember that

95

when you thought I had sent for you, you came, even if suspiciously."

"Good night, Nan," he said. "And don't ask any more questions, and be careful what you hear, or you're apt to find yourself in trouble."

She looked at him for a moment; then she put her hands on his shoulders and leaned forward to kiss him lightly on the lips.

"Be careful yourself," she said. "Even if I won't marry you, I don't want you killed."

He grinned. "I'll keep it in mind," he said, and went out.

18

COMING DOWN the stairs, Colonel Paradine gave a quick glance toward the dining room, from which came the sounds of dishes and silverware being arranged in preparation for breakfast. The Colonel walked swiftly down the hall and took his hat from the stand by the door, but he could not help pausing for a moment before the nearby mirror, as was his habit. He smoothed his light mustache with a forefinger, and set the hat upon his head, adjusting the angle of it carefully; then he turned to the door. His daughter's voice, behind him, made him start guiltily and release the knob.

"Dad!" She came running down the hall toward him, making a pretty picture in her light, blue-flowered dress. "You were leaving without your breakfast!" she said in a surprised voice, after reaching him. "It's all ready. I was just about to have Teresa call you."

"I'm sorry, my dear," he said. "I have to get to the bank. I'll get something to eat later, at the café down the street."

"Oh," she said, and looked at him closely, and went on in a changed and hardened voice, "You're avoiding me, aren't you, Dad? Well, it isn't necessary. Francis was happy to tell me all about it. So come have your breakfast."

The Colonel said weakly, "My dear, I don't know what you're—"

"The marshal was here yesterday afternoon, wasn't he? About Boyd. And you told him you had no idea where Boyd had managed to get his hands on ten thousand dollars. Why, Dad? Because you've decided to take a dislike to Boyd? It's very easy to hate somebody to whom you're indebted, isn't it?"

"I've told you I don't consider myself—"

"Then why did you lie to the marshal, Dad?" Her voice was sharp. "If you don't hate Boyd or feel indebted to him, why make trouble for him with the law?"

"For a young lady engaged to be married, you're showing a great deal of concern about a man other than your husband, my dear."

"Oh, fiddlesticks!" she said. "I'm a member of this family, aren't I? I try to tell myself I'm proud of it; I try to tell myself that it's all right to forget what happened when I was just a baby and just remember the pleasant things that have happened since, few though they are. But it's getting pretty hard for me to fool myself, Dad. Boyd Cohoon's behavior since he got back may have been inexcusable, but what about ours? Oh, I'm not pretending to be guiltless; I had a part in it, too. Boyd did a fine thing for us, and how have we repaid him? I'll tell you how! First I cheated him of what he had every right to expect, and then Francis tried to have him killed, and now you lie about him. . . . Why, Dad, why?"

The Colonel looked down at the erect, diminutive figure of his daughter with a feeling that was frighteningly close to hatred: they never let him forget it, he thought bitterly, never for a moment; whenever anything went wrong, anything whatsoever, it was always his fault because of what he had done—for their sakes—twenty years ago. Elinor with her illnesses, Francis with his women and drinking, and now this righteous slip of a girl in an expensive New York dress for which he had recently paid the bill, chattering of family pride—how much pride would she have been able to afford if he had not acted as he had? Other girls of her generation had starved and gone barefoot—yes, and sold themselves to Yankee carpetbaggers for the price of a meal.

He tried to express his anger and resentment, but as usual the words would not come. What he said, was, weakly, "I can't explain, my dear. It's not that I really have anything personal against the fellow, although, as you say, his conduct has been inexcusable. But there are reasons . . ."

"Reasons!" Claire said hotly. "I can think of only one, that you're afraid of what people will think, Paul in particular, if they learn we gave Boyd that much money. . . . Or is there another?" She looked up, startled at some thought, to regard her parent closely. "Are you afraid to have it known

97

that you gave away ten thousand dollars because somebody might ask where you got it?"

"Claire!"

"Well, where did you get it, Dad?" the girl demanded quickly. "Just a week or two ago you were complaining because all our money was tied up in mining stocks." Her voice was a whisper now; and her eyes never left his face. "I see. You paid our debt to Boyd Cohoon in one big, generous gesture—with other people's money! Oh, Dad," she cried softly, "what kind of people are we? What's going to become of us?"

The Colonel cleared his throat to speak, and had to clear it again. "I . . . don't know where you got this fantastic notion, young lady, and I suggest you dismiss it instantly. The money was obtained quite legitimately, and it will be repaid as soon as I can liquidate a few of my investments. Considering the fact that it was used to free you from an unpleasant obligation, my dear, I consider your attitude unfair and unreasonable, as well as ungrateful."

He turned and marched out of the house, feeling pleased with himself for having had the last word. Outside, windblown dust greeted him, and bright sunlight. He walked quickly away, lest his daughter call him back and spoil his exit. As he turned the corner, he had to step aside to avoid collision with a rough-looking individual in worn range clothing.

"You'd be Mr. Paradine?"

The Colonel stopped. "I'm Colonel Paradine."

"Mr. Westerman wants you in his office."

The summons had a peremptory sound that was offensive to the Colonel in his present mood. "Indeed?" he said. "You can tell Mr. Westerman—"

"Tell him yourself," the man said. "It's running back and forth between the two of you all day I'd be if I started bearing messages in that tone of voice. Good day, Colonel."

Colonel Paradine looked after the broad, retreating back of the man with indignation: the attitude of these people—their lack of respect for position and family—was as insufferable as their climate. Twenty years had not developed in the Colonel any liking for this land of his exile. Although he tired of his wife's complaints on the subject, he could not but admit that they were basically justified. Now he struck his cane into the ground, and continued his walk, reaching Main Street at the familiar corner and making a smart, military right turn, as was his daily custom. Gradually, however, his pace slowed. Finally he looked around, although it had not been his intention to do so. His glance picked out the hotel, taller than the other edifices along the street, and the shabby building opposite with the shaded second-floor windows. He found that he had come to a halt. He sighed, about-faced, and strode back down the street.

Westerman greeted him at the office door. "I'm sorry to take up your time, sir," the younger man said with soothing deference. "However, in view of the unfortunate situation at the Lucky Seven, I thought we'd better—"

The Colonel felt a spasm of fear contract the muscles of his throat. "The Lucky Seven? Is something wrong at the mine, Paul?"

Westerman closed the door, and turned the key in the lock. "Please be seated, Colonel," he said, walking to his desk. "No, I wouldn't say the trouble was *at* the mine, exactly. The loss of the payroll three nights ago was quite a blow. I'm trying to raise the money, but meanwhile the men still haven't been paid. And now young Cohoon has laid down an ultimatum"—Westerman picked up a legal-appearing document and tapped it against the palm of his left hand —"refusing us passage across the Grant unless we pay him an exorbitant toll for every ton of ore hauled. Here, would you like to read it, sir?"

The Colonel waved the paper aside. "But . . . but isn't there something—"

"Oh, we could take it to court, of course—those old Spanish land titles are always somewhat shaky—but it would cost money. I suppose we could use force, but I hesitate to do so under the circumstances. If Cohoon were to be killed in a fight with our men, people would remember how his father and brother died, and suspect us of having engineered all three deaths just to make an easy haul for our ore. It doesn't pay to disregard public opinion entirely; you never know what's going to turn a bunch of peaceful citizens into an angry mob." The small man behind the big desk shrugged his shoulders regretfully. "So I see no alternative to closing down the mine, at least for a while."

"Closing it down!" Colonel Paradine gasped. "But you can't—" He checked himself. "Isn't there some other way of getting the ore out?"

Westerman said dryly, "Certainly. We can carry it over the Candelarias by pack mule. Or we can haul north over Yellow Ford and Sombrero, a two-day detour for the wagons under the best conditions. We tried that before, when the vein was considerably richer than it is now, and barely broke even. No, Sir, I'm afraid there's no choice. The mine will have to shut down. I thought, as a matter of friendship, I'd let you know a little in advance."

The Colonel's mind was working clearly now, after the initial shock, and he asked, "A little? How much time do I have? I was planning to sell—"

Westerman was shaking his head regretfully. "I'd like to do it, sir, but you can see how it would look, if I gave my future father-in-law time to dispose of his stock. There's really no need to be alarmed, Colonel. The silver's still there. Given a little time, we'll find a way of getting it out at a profit; you won't lose your money." He hesitated, and went on, "Of course, if you're in immediate need of funds, I'll be happy to personally advance you whatever you need, with the stock as security, just to prove how much faith I have in the Lucky Seven."

"Well, I hate to take advantage of your generosity, Paul. I already owe you—"

"Ah, think nothing of it. I'm glad to be of service; and it's all in the family, isn't it?" There was something faintly unpleasant about Westerman's smile, but the Colonel chose to disregard it. The younger man went on: "Just name the figure, sir. . . ."

It was always a distasteful business, borrowing money; and Colonel Paradine got through it as fast as possible, scrawling his signature at the bottom of the paper Westerman put before him, after glancing through it hastily—not that he did not trust the other man, but there was never any harm in being careful what you signed. Westerman went out of the room and, after a time, came back with a small satchel, which, opened by the Colonel, proved to contain the required sum in gold and bank notes.

"Well," he said, rising, "thank you very much, Paul. I certainly appreciate this. I'll see you at the house tonight, I hope?"

Westerman did not answer immediately. The expression on his face was odd and far from reassuring; the Colonel looked away, found his hat and cane, moved to the door, and glanced back to find the other still watching him in that peculiar and offensive way.

"Well," Colonel Paradine said, "well, I must be leaving—"

"Go straight to the bank," Westerman said. "That money goes into the bank, Colonel. Nowhere else."

Colonel Paradine stared at him in amazement. "Really, Paul, I—"

"You old fool," Westerman said softly. "Do you think I've nursed you along this far, just to have you smash everything by your stupidity? Get that money into the bank and straighten up your affairs before somebody gets wind of the situation. Do you think I've worked this long and climbed this high only to wind up with a wife whose father went to prison for pilfering from the funds entrusted to his care? I need Claire, Colonel, and I need you, and I need the bank; they're all part of my plans, and I'm not going to have them broken and dirtied by your clumsiness. Now get out of here. . . . Wait a minute! Let's get things straight between us, once and for all. Do you really think I don't know why you gave ten thousand dollars to Boyd Cohoon? Do you think that in five years I haven't managed to learn who really rode with my son Harry the day he was killed? I was deceived for a while, I admit; and it was convenient to keep on acting deceived. It gave me a public motive for hating young Cohoon, in case I should need one; and it made possible my courtship of your daughter, which would have been awkward otherwise. But I've known the true story for years, Colonel. It gave me an added reason for wanting Claire to be my wife. It seems only fair, doesn't it, that since the Paradines cost me a son, they should supply one?"

The Colonel listened to the soft, mocking voice in a kind of paralysis of shock; then it stopped. He heard himself make a kind of choked, roaring sound; and he was plunging forward blindly with his cane raised. Arms closed on him from behind, holding him powerless. If anything could have added to the humiliation of the moment, it would have been this: to be held kicking and struggling, helpless as an angry child. He stopped fighting the bearded man who had seized him.

"All right, Rudy." Westerman had not smiled at the spectacle. "Come to your senses, Colonel," he said. "If you did succeed in killing me with that stick, you'd be a ruined man. You need me even worse than I need you. Now get that money into the bank and let me know if you need more to cover. . . ." He stopped speaking abruptly, and turned to the nearest open window, through which came the sound of gunfire, close at hand.

19

AFTER HER FATHER'S angry departure, Claire Paradine had remained standing in the front hall for a time, shamed and frightened by what the interview had revealed, not only about her parent, but about herself as well, and her family as a whole. *Why,* she thought, *we're none of us any good. We lie and cheat and rob and kill; we're hypocrites living respectably on broken promises and stolen money!* She heard her mother's voice upstairs, querulous and demanding. Automatically she started for the stairs; then she turned instead, snatched up a shawl and flung it over her head in the Spanish manner, and fled from the house.

It was hot and bright and windy outside. She walked quickly toward Main Street while the decision formed in her mind. At the corner she had to pause and turn her back to a sudden gust that filled the air with fine sand and threatened to lift her skirts to indecorous heights. When it had subsided, she started to walk rapidly toward the hotel, beyond which was the small building that housed the marshal's office and jail.

Her resolve was strong for the first few steps, but presently it faltered, as it began to seem unfair of her to do what she had in mind without at least letting her father know so that he could take some action to protect himself. After all, if he was actually in trouble at the bank, it was at least partly on her account, as he had said—although he had doubtless also been motivated by the desire to have nothing interfere with her profitable marriage to Paul Westerman; also, he was childishly fond of flamboyant gestures, particularly those involving impressive sums of money. . . .

Claire found that she had come to a halt; then she was hurrying back along the street toward the bank. The building was still cool from the night when she entered it. Francis was nowhere to be seen, which was a relief; she had no desire to explain her errand to her brother. John Fergus, at his window, informed her that her father, also, had not yet come in; and it occurred to her that, having missed breakfast at home, he might have stopped on the way for something to eat.

The delay was annoying, as was young Fergus's eagerness to be of service. She went into the rear office to sit down and wait in peace. It was from there that she heard the harsh, accented voice order the people outside to put up their hands. She was standing up, looking about her for a means of escaping from the room to run for help—the lone window was barred—when the door was thrown open by a masked man with a gun, who dragged her by the arm out onto the bank floor where, feeling as if caught in a kind of nightmare, she found herself lined up against a wall with the tellers and half a dozen customers, while the robbers systematically went about their business.

There were four of them inside the building, she saw, all masked. The leader, who held two guns on the prisoners, was a plump man of medium height, dressed in a colorful uniform liberally adorned with gold lace. Claire regarded him with fearful interest: this, then, was the notorious General. It was a little difficult to take him seriously in that gaudy costume; these Mexican bandits and generals—the terms were often interchangeable—always looked a little as if they were acting a part on a stage. At least this was the impression Claire had gained from what she had read and heard; and the comic-opera appearance of the man by the door did nothing to refute the idea. The guns in his hands, however, were steady and sobering, dispelling any notion that he was not in deadly earnest.

Beside him stood a somewhat taller man, wearing a large black hat, a close-fitting embroidered black jacket, and tight black trousers. The fancy costume, as well as the black mask, gave this one, too, and air of unreality except for the rifle under his arm. The other two bandits were more shabbily and conventionally dressed.

A shot in the street made the two by the door glance at each other quickly. The General murmured a soft phrase, and the other, clearly the second in command, stepped forward.

"Hurry it up there, *amigos!*" he snapped. "Must we spend all the day in this place?"

"The vault is locked, Señor." The speaker, Claire noted, was the outlaw who had so unceremoniously dragged her out of her father's office; a thin, dark individual with a shambling gait and a thick, slurred voice.

The black-clad one said, "Well, unlock it, fool!"

"But, Señor, I do not have the key."

Outside, the single shot had been followed by sporadic

firing, mostly, it seemed, by men stationed outside the bank. They were not entirely unopposed, however; at the front of the room a window shattered with a tinkling sound as a bullet from across the street carried away part of the frame.

The General spoke again, in an undertone, and his lieutenant said harshly, "Must we then always have to work with drunkards and imbeciles? Come here and stand guard." He waited for the other to take his place beside the General; then he walked slowly toward the prisoners. Abruptly he halted and swung the rifle-barrel to cover freckled young John Fergus. "You," he said, "open the vault."

Fergus instinctively started forward to obey, but checked himself, and squared his shoulders in an obstinate manner. "Open it yourself!"

"I will count to five," said the black-clad lieutenant. "Then I will shoot you and see if your associate, beside you, is equally stubborn. If you both die without speaking, there is always dynamite. I start the count now: one, two, three. . . ." The rifle, already cocked, steadied for the shot.

"Johnny!" Claire Paradine heard herself cry. "For Heaven's sake, open it, Johnny!"

Fergus sighed. "Very well, Miss Paradine," he said. "If you say so." His face was pale beneath the freckles. He turned and moved away, followed closely by the bandit lieutenant.

Claire leaned against the wall, shaken. Instinct told her that death had been very close—and the firing outside was growing in intensity. It would be utterly stupid, she reflected, to be killed by a bullet from the gun of someone she had known all her life, but it was a decided possibility, the reckless way they seemed to be shooting at the windows without any regard for those unfortunate enough to be caught inside. . . . The robbery seemed to have gone on forever, and she found herself swaying where she stood. A ricocheting bullet from outside came moaning across the room and struck the wall directly above her, showering her with dust and causing her to bite cruelly into her lip to keep from screaming.

At last the fourth man—a stocky individual of medium height—came running from the vault to speak to someone at the door; two more men came inside to help with the bags into which the money had been loaded; and they began to leave. The second-in-command came back into sight still holding his gun on young Fergus, whom he waved back into line among the prisoners. The General, still holding his guns ready, stepped aside to let the laden men pass, and collided with the man beside him.

The impact threw the General off balance. He stumbled, and one leg seemed to give way under the strain; he caught himself with an odd, skipping little jump, and pivoted to cover the prisoners, none of whom had had time to move. It was a meaningless incident, over too quickly for anyone to have taken advantage of it, even if the lieutenant had not been standing by with a cocked rifle. The man who had been the involuntary cause of it murmured an apology; the General jerked his head toward the street, and the man went out. The black-clad lieutenant moved over to join the General, and the two of them waited until the last man from the vault had gone outside. Then the General spoke to the lieutenant, still in that soft undertone that was inaudible across the room.

The man beside him shifted the rifle under his left arm. He looked at the prisoners, and said, "The next time we pay you a visit, *amigos*, do not annoy us with stubborn delays." His freed right hand rose, caught a weapon hidden at the nape of his neck, and snapped down smartly. A pinwheel of light seemed to span the room; and John Fergus clutched at his chest and crumpled to the floor in a terrible, inert manner. Claire saw him die and was horrified and grieved—after all, the boy had been in love with her—but she could spare him only a glance, and not even that for his murderer. Her attention remained fixed on the gaudily costumed figure in the doorway.

She had been staring incredulously ever since that curious little stumble and recovery, remembering someone whose leg had been smashed by a bullet five years before. Now she saw the masked General look directly at her; and even as she told herself that this was insane, she knew that the hair beneath the gold-trimmed uniform cap would be fair, and the eyes in the shadow of the visor, blue—as blue as her own. She knew also that the man by the door had seen the recognition on her face. She saw the guns he held lift and come steady, and she knew a moment of utter terror. *No, oh, no!* she cried silently, *I won't tell; I'll never tell, I promise. . . .*

The General laughed—the sound muffled by his mask—and turned away. Claire watched until the doorway was empty; then, to the sound of running horses and redoubled firing outside, she fainted.

20

Nan Montoya had fallen into the habit of sleeping until noon to make up for the late hours at Miss Bessie's. The sound of men's voices in the outer room, and Jesusa's angry outcry, awakened her from a kind of morning half-slumber. She slipped out of bed, pulled on a robe to cover her night-dress, and snatched up Montoya's little gun. There seemed to be a struggle immediately outside her room, and Jesusa was shouting to her in Spanish to flee by the back door—although she did not understand the individual words, the meaning was clear.

Nan looked down at her gun in her hand, determined how to cock the weapon, did so, and, brushing the blanket aside, stepped through the doorway. Jesusa was engaged in an uneven struggle with three men who were trying warily to deprive her of her knife. There were more men by the front door. Marshal Black was standing a little apart, with the look of a man performing a necessary but distasteful duty.

Nan aimed her gun at him.

"Tell them to stop, Marshal. Tell them to let her go!"

Black stiffened at the threat of the small weapon. "Put that gun down, ma'am. I represent the law—"

His pompous tones, and the sound of a blow followed by a cry of pain from Jesusa, snapped Nan's temper off short. She had been about to speak; instead, she slanted the revolver slightly downwards, sighting along the barrel, and pulled the trigger. The report was deafening under the low roof. The bullet struck closer to the marshal than she had intended; dirt from the floor sprayed over his boots.

The shot was followed by complete silence, which she broke by recocking her weapon, using both hands.

"Now take your law and get out of here, Mr. Black," she said quietly. "And tell the man who's sneaking through my bedroom that if he takes another step I'll pull this trigger again; and this time I'm not aiming at the floor." The sound of movement behind her did not stop; and she gripped the gun more tightly. "I mean that!"

"All right, Mallory," the marshal said reluctantly to the

man in the bedroom. "And you men, let that woman go."
He looked at Nan. "Miss Montoya—"

"Mrs. Montoya!"

"Mrs. Montoya, you're obstructing justice. We're looking
for Boyd Cohoon—"

She made her voice even. "Well, go look for him somewhere else. He isn't here."

"Could you tell us—"

"I'll tell nothing to a bunch of ruffians who burst into my
house without knocking. If you want any information from
me, send this mob outside. . . ." The word, used without
thought, startled her as she realized that this *was* a mob; a
lynch mob. Their set faces held a look of cruel anticipation
that she recognized without ever having seen it before.

Black was saying, "You don't understand, ma'am. It's a
matter of—"

"I don't care what it's a matter of!" she snapped, forcing
herself to maintain the role she had assumed. "Either mend
your manners or get your information elsewhere."

Somebody said in a surly voice, "We need no lessons in
manners from the likes of—"

Black saw the danger signals in her face, and cut in
quickly: "Tell us just this, ma'am. Did you see Cohoon last
night?"

"Yes."

"And do you know where he was headed when he left
you?"

She had gained herself time enough, now, to know how to
answer this question. "Yes."

"And will you tell me—"

"I'll tell you nothing more until you get this herd of buffalo out of my house!"

The soberly clad young man with the badge studied her
for a moment; she could see the formed judgment in his
eyes. To William Black there would be only two kinds of
women—good women, to be humbly worshipped from afar,
and the kind of women who worked on Creek Lane. She had
met the attitude often enough that she should have become
hardened to it, but it never failed to anger her. She spoke to
him, therefore, as if to an undisciplined boy.

"Try coming in again, Marshal. This time, try knocking."

He hesitated; then he bowed. "Very well, ma'am." The
fact that he could so swallow his pride was a disturbing
measure of the man and his purpose. Nan watched him turn
and speak to the other men; there was a short battle of wills,

and they filed sullenly through the door. Black followed them outside.

Nan found herself trembling, but there was no time for this. She spoke reassuringly to Jesusa; then hurried into the bedroom. It was empty but the door leading outside stood open. She went to her trunk, threw the lid up, and found the box of cartridges she had inherited with the gun she was holding. It took her a moment to work out the proper method of opening the weapon so that she could reload the fired chamber. Men made a big mystery of things like this, she reflected, and there was undoubtedly more to handling a gun than loading and cocking it, and making it discharge in the general direction desired; but on the whole it seemed like a fairly simple mechanism that, for all practical purposes, any fool could master. . . . She kept her mind on the business at hand, shutting out all thought of Boyd Cohoon. Panicky guesses would not help him.

Knuckles rapped on the front door. She dropped the fully loaded gun into the pocket of her robe, and went to let the marshal in. He was alone: but in the moment before the door closed behind him, she saw that the others had not gone far. There seemed to be more of them than there had been.

Black turned to face her. "Ma'am, the men are pretty short of patience—"

"I know," she said. "They'd like to beat the information out of me, wouldn't they? Maybe even hang me. Mobs aren't particular who they get, I understand."

"Mrs. Montoya, this is a regularly organized posse, and the men out there have all been legally deputized—"

"All right," she said. "Tell me, what's Cohoon done that's so terrible?"

"It's no joke, Mrs. Montoya. The General held up the bank half an hour ago; and a man was murdered in cold blood. You must have heard the shooting."

"If I let a little shooting bother me in this town," Nan said, "I'd never get any sleep. So now you've decided to pin this Mexican bandit's crimes on Boyd Cohoon, Marshal? Despite the fact that the General's been operating pretty steadily for several years, all of which time Cohoon's been in prison? I understand there's bad blood between you. It must be nice to wear a badge and be able to point the law at anybody you don't happen to like."

Black flushed. "My personal feelings aren't involved," he said stiffly. "Nor are we trying to pin anything on Cohoon that doesn't belong there. The General will answer for his own crimes in due time. But Cohoon, acting as his lieutenant, killed a man this morning, murdered him deliberately and without provocation, on a word from his chief. Witnesses have identified the knife as well as the man who threw it—"

"The knife!" Nan said quickly. "Is that your evidence, Cohoon's knife?" She laughed. "Marshal, if your gun was used to kill a man, would it necessarily follow that you were guilty of murder? Cohoon was lured into the alley next to the Double Eagle last night by someone using my name. He lost his knife and gun in the fight—you don't have to take my word for it. Just ask Miss Bessie or anybody who was there and saw him come in; ask at Flagler's, somebody there went out with a lantern while the fight was going on. Cohoon threw his knife to smash the lantern; that's how it was lost. I went out afterwards to look. His gun and hat were still there, but the knife was gone."

Black had listened to her with silent patience; now he shook his head, almost sadly. "Whether he lost it or not last night doesn't matter, ma'am; he had it today at the bank. The knife is just corroborative evidence, anyway. I tell you, Mrs. Montoya, he was recognized and identified in spite of his fancy costume; there's no possible doubt—"

"I don't believe it," Nan said curtly. "You mean he helped rob a bank full of people, and killed a man, without even taking the precaution of wearing a mask?"

"Oh, he was masked, but a witness recognized him anyway—"

"What witness?"

"Mrs. Montoya, we're wasting time! If you know where Boyd Cohoon can be found, it's your duty to tell me."

Nan looked at him for a moment; the man was clearly at the end of his patience. He would tell her nothing more. She sighed, as if accepting defeat.

"Well, I suppose you're right, although I'm sure your witness was mistaken. Boyd wouldn't . . ." She hesitated, feigning reluctance, and continued presently: "He told me . . . he told me he was riding over into the Candaleria Mountains by way of Yellow Ford, wherever that is. He wanted to investigate a mine owned by Mr. Westerman, I don't know why. He didn't say. That's all I know." She glanced at the marshal quickly. "You'll see that he gets a fair trial, won't you?"

"Yes," Black said, "of course, Ma'am. Thank you for the information."

She opened the door for him; when he had gone, she

closed it and leaned against it, suddenly dizzy and trembling. She tried to think clearly, but all that came to her was the memory of her own voice saying, *There will be no messenger from me.* Pride, and also concern for his safety, had led her to arrange matters so that Cohoon would believe no one she might send to him; he would only sense another trap, even in a genuine warning. It followed that she would have to go herself. She closed and locked the door.

"Jesusa," she said softly, "Jesusa, can you tell me how to get to—"

The old woman shook her fist at the locked door, through which her assailants had recently departed, and embarked upon a stream of imprecations in Spanish that flowed too rapidly for Nan to have deciphered it even had she known all the terms employed.

"Jesusa!" Nan cried impatiently. "Jesusa, please! Can you get somebody to guide me . . . ?"

Unhearing, the old woman continued to recite her litany of hate, rocking back and forth on the stool by the fireplace. Nan regarded her with wry helplessness, and went quickly into the other room to the open trunk and began to search through its contents heedlessly. She tried not to think of how little she was prepared for the responsibility that had been thrust upon her: the responsibility for a man's life. It had been years since she had mounted a horse; and she knew nothing of this country except what she had seen from the stage. She remembered it as beautiful but rather terrifying; the kind of country in which a lone and inexperienced rider could lose himself without a trace. *I'll need water,* she thought, *a horse, water, a gun, and clear directions. Can I trust Miss Bessie?*

She weighed the risks in her mind as she took from the bottom of the trunk the fashionable green riding habit she had packed away upon the eve of running off to be married. She remembered having had some pretty picture in mind of herself and Montoya riding side by side across their California rancho—not that he had ever claimed to be a rancher, you had to give him credit for that much. Well, Montoya was dead, and whatever she had felt for him was dead with him. Dead men and dead emotions could take care of themselves. . . .

A peremptory knock on the front door interrupted her. She glanced around quickly, dumped the riding clothes back into the trunk and threw some other garments on top of them, and walked swiftly into the other room, feeling for the revolver that was still heavy in her pocket. Waving Jesusa back, she approached the door, and turned the key in the lock, lefthanded.

"*Now* what do you want?" she called as she did so. "Haven't you pestered me enough for one morning. . . ."

The door swung open under her hand. Instead of Marshal Black or one of his associates, as she had expected, she found herself confronted by a small, fair, bareheaded girl in a blue-flowered dress. The two women faced each other in silence for a moment. Nan was startled to note that, in addition to lacking hat or bonnet, her visitor was noticeably disheveled; but the smaller girl's forlorn appearance was not due entirely to the untidiness of her hair and the dust on her garments. Her face was shockingly pale; and her eyes had the pink, swollen look of tears, both shed and unshed.

"I . . . I'm looking for Mrs. Montoya."

"I'm Mrs. Montoya," Nan said. "You're Claire Paradine. That takes care of the formalities. Come inside, Miss Paradine. You don't want to ruin your reputation by being seen visiting on this street." She stepped aside to let the other pass.

"Please lock the door," Claire Paradine said.

"It's locked."

The smaller girl turned to look at Nan. "Mrs. Montoya," she said, "Mrs. Montoya, I've got to get a message to Boyd Cohoon. It's a matter of life and death. Can you get in touch with him?"

Nan studied the pale, pinched face for a moment. "You're the second person to come looking for him within the hour. The first was the marshal. Why should I tell you more than I did him?"

"I tell you, it's a matter of—"

"I know," Nan said. "Life and death. What's the message, Miss Paradine?"

"If the marshal's already been here, you ought to be able to guess!" Claire Paradine cried breathlessly. "I want you to warn Boyd; you've got to warn him! They . . . they're like wild animals; you should have seen them at the bank! If they catch him, they'll hang him without a trial. I heard them laughing about it as they rode off. *Laughing!*" She buried her face in her hands.

Nan said quietly, "This concern for Cohoon's welfare seems to have come over you very suddenly, Miss Paradine. From what I hear, you showed few signs of it when he first came back. Have you now decided that you want him, after all?"

"No," the smaller girl gasped, "I mean, I don't know. I

mean . . . Oh, it isn't that at all. You don't understand. Please, you must warn him. I couldn't stand it if he were killed. I simply couldn't stand it. I'd just die!" She looked up, and her eyes were wide and dark. "You see . . . you see, I lied about him."

"You what?" Nan stared at her visitor in growing comprehension. "*You* were the witness? *You* identified the murderer as . . ." She took a step forward, and Claire Paradine shrank back, crying:

"I couldn't help it! They were all around me; they wanted to know if I'd recognized . . . anybody. I didn't know what they meant. I thought . . . They saw I'd seen *something*."

"What?" Nan asked.

Claire Paradine did not look at her. "It was horrible," she cried. "People I'd known all my life, pushing and pulling at me as if they wanted to tear me apart! If it hadn't been for the marshal, I declare I think they'd have ripped the clothes right off my back. I didn't know what they were driving at. I thought . . ."

"What did you think?" Nan demanded harshly.

"I couldn't help it, I tell you!" Claire Paradine gasped. "They showed me the knife, and it was Boyd's knife. It *was!* I didn't lie about that. I'd seen his father wearing it often enough. Then they wanted me to say it was Boyd; they *told* me to say it was Boyd—the man who had thrown it. And he *was* dark and just about the same size; but I tried to tell them . . . They thought I was shielding him. Even the marshal, who'd been protecting me, got angry. . . . I *did* try to tell them," she whimpered. "I did, but they wouldn't listen. They just kept at me until I said . . . until I said . . ." Abruptly she sank to her knees beside the nearby cot and pressed her face against the coarse blanket, weeping.

Nan looked down grimly; it was no time for anger or hate or even contempt, but she had to fight back the impulse to give the smaller girl a hard kick in the locality that was temptingly vulnerable as she knelt there. She thought of Boyd Cohoon, who had given up a large fraction of his life for this girl—but that was his business. There was a germ of an idea in the thought, however, and she remembered Cohoon's voice, the night before, saying teasingly, *She can probably ride better and shoot straighter than you.*

Nan turned the notion over in her mind; it pointed a way out of the dilemma posed by her own poor horsemanship and lack of knowledge of the country. Claire Paradine could undoubtedly find her way to Willow Spring unaided; and Cohoon would believe her warning. There was bitterness in that, and Nan spoke to herself sharply: *If you go yourself, you'll have nothing but his gratitude, even if you manage to find him in time. If you sent her—if they're alone out there together—who knows? Try it and see.*

She heard herself laugh coldly. "That's a lovely story, and you must be very proud of yourself, Miss Paradine, but why tell me about it?"

The smaller girl raised her head quickly, "Why, you can warn him—"

Nan laughed again. "*I* warn him? Not me, dearie. Even if I was prepared to risk my life out on that godforsaken desert of yours for Boyd Cohoon, I wouldn't interfere with the law. A girl in my profession keeps on the good side of the law, or she starves to death very quickly."

"The law!" Claire Paradine cried scornfully. "They're nothing but a mob of drunken hoodlums—"

"Whom you have sent out to hang a man," Nan said. "I'll do this much, and no more! I'll tell you where to find him. He's heading for a place on his ranch called Willow Spring, by way of Black's Ferry. I told the marshal he went the other way, but I doubt if he believed me; however, I figure that takes care of any debt I owe Cohoon. You can warn him or let him be lynched as you please."

Claire Paradine got slowly to her feet. "Why, I thought you and Boyd . . . He gave you money, didn't he?"

"Other men have given me money, Miss Paradine. Let me worry about my conscience. You just take care of yours. Now get out of here."

The smaller girl hesitated; then she walked quickly to the door, fought the lock briefly, and ran out. After a moment Nan moved into the open doorway to watch the small, blue-clad figure make its hurried way up the street, attracting the attention of the few loafers awake at this hour of the morning—it was a part of town that lived mainly at night.

Suddenly Claire Paradine came to a halt. She stood for a moment in the center of the street, as if making a decision. She turned on her heel and marched into the space between two buildings—one a small tavern—and came out leading a saddled horse. The long stirrups, and her hampering dress, made it difficult for her to mount, but she reached the saddle on the third try and was off at a gallop, as a man came running out of the tavern to stare in amazement, forgetting the drawn revolver in his hand.

21

COLONEL PARADINE stood in the center of the bank floor, facing his questioners with what he hoped looked to them like calm assurance.

"Yes, sir," he said to a worried face before him, "funds to cover the loss will be here within the week; there's no cause for alarm, none at all. . . . Yes, indeed, Mrs. Purvis," he said, "all depositors will be paid in full if they so wish. . . . What is it, sir?"

A big man in dusty range clothing had pushed through the knot of people. This individual spoke curtly:

"Your name's Paradine?"

"I'm Colonel Paradine, yes. What can I do for you?"

"You owe me a horse," the stranger said.

The Colonel frowned. "If you'd be so kind as to explain. . . ."

"I had **him** standing in the alley by McCordley's bar, not wishing to leave him in the sun. I heard a noise and stepped to the door; a girl was riding off with him, hell for leather. Had it been a man, I'd have shot him out of the saddle. Being as it was a woman, I didn't. She was small, blonde, wearing a light-blue dress; people tell me she's your daughter. I could make trouble, but I'll settle for the price of the horse and gear."

Colonel Paradine sensed a stir among the people surrounding him. His calm bearing had partially restored their confidence in him; but it had vanished again with this reminder of the part Claire had played in their common disaster. It still seemed incredible to the Colonel that his daughter should have tried to shield Cohoon, refusing to identify him until shown the incontrovertible evidence of his guilt. She had always been a sensible girl; but now there were even those who, encouraged by her strange behavior, had the temerity to suggest that she had acted as the man's accomplice throughout—after all, it was she who had ordered poor young Fergus to open the vault. And after all this, to steal a horse and ride out of town in such a conspicuous manner—had the girl gone insane? And where was Francis in this terrible hour?

It seemed to the Colonel as if the whole world had become afflicted with sudden madness, particularly his own family.

He drew himself up. "I apologize for my daughter, sir," he said. This was no time to get into an argument; and the stranger was armed and had a hardbitten look about him. Colonel Paradine reached into his pocket, counted out a sum of money and, with his inability to resist a fine gesture, added an equal amount to it. "There you are; I think you'll find it adequate."

The stranger took the money, and made his own count with infuriating deliberation. "Three hundred," he said, and looked up and grinned. "It's a deal, Paradine. At that price, I'd sell you a dozen more, if I had them. Well, give my regards to the young lady. I'll say this for her: she looked better on that pony than I ever did."

He touched the brim of his hat in a mock salute, and walked off; the crowd let him through, and closed in again, openly hostile now. His magnanimous gesture had been a mistake, the Colonel realized; with their savings in jeopardy, these people did not like to see him casually pay out three hundred dollars for a drifter's broken-down horse and worn-out saddle. It put the thought in their minds that he might have been as careless with their money as he was with his own.

Their faces frightened him, and he spoke quickly, "As I was saying, your deposits will be repaid to the last cent, even if it takes everything I possess. You have my word on it. Now, if you'll excuse me—"

For a moment he thought they would refuse to let him go; then they opened a path for him. As he walked away, he heard the murmur of their voices behind him, sullen and suspicious—that was the fault of Claire and her incomprehensible behavior, he thought bitterly. What had the girl been doing in the bank, anyway? If it had not been for her, there would have been no thought of mistrust. He would have had time and privacy, particularly with young Fergus gone. The catastrophe might even have been turned into a blessing of sorts. At least, he could have straightened out the books; with so much money missing, who could ever have found the discrepancies? But now, with everyone watching him suspiciously, it was out of the question. They would discover his peculations; and shortly they would learn that his promises of repayment were only empty words. . . .

He was aware of greeting passersby as he walked, and pausing to speak reassuringly; and he was filled with wonder and admiration for the part of his mind that could still function in the face of ruin. Then he was in the house with the door shut behind him; and it was safe to let his face relax, at last, into lines of exhaustion and despair. He stumbled into the study and fell into his chair and covered his face with his hands. After a while he sat up slowly, as the thought came into his mind that there was only one honorable course for a man to take in such a situation.

The Colonel's hand found the drawer pull, and located the worn, efficient butt of the big revolver. The weapon had never been reloaded since its return by Cohoon, but it still held two charges, one more than necessary. The Colonel drew it out, cocked it, raised it, and lowered it again; a shudder went through him. He laid the weapon aside, rose, and walked quickly to the safe in the corner, opened this, and took out a small packet similar to that which he had once given to Cohoon. Looking at it, he regretted that generosity, and even more he regretted the satchel Paul Westerman had returned to his safe, pointing out that it would be inadvisable for the Colonel to make his appearance at the bank, under the circumstances, carrying a bag full of money. Colonel Paradine, being a realist, had no hope of ever seeing that money again; Westerman was not the type to show generosity to a disgraced and broken man who could be of no further use to him. There would be no further loans, and no marriage.

The Colonel laid the paper-wrapped packet gently on the desk. It was not a drop to what he owed—not to mention what people would expect him to repay, even if he could not be held legally responsible. Yet it was enough to take him away from this miserable place, west to California perhaps, where an enterprising and intelligent man with a small stake could surely make the fortune he deserved. . . .

"Where are we going this time?"

He looked up, startled by the sound of his wife's voice. She was standing on the far side of the desk, fully dressed, watching him.

"Elinor—"

She said quietly, "You're in trouble again, aren't you, Roger? Well, which direction do we flee this time? Have you another desert in mind, where we can spend the next twenty years? Or perhaps it's to be a tropical jungle this time." She looked at the packet of bank notes. "How much are you stealing this time, Roger? Whose trust are you betraying this time? Besides mine, I mean?"

He crouched there, held by the deathly calm of her voice.

He did not move until she reached for the gun on the desk; and then it was too late.

The servants came running at the sound of the shot; but they had not reached the door before a second report revived the echoes of the first.

22

COHOON HAD followed the road for a while after leaving town the previous night, but he had pulled off it a distance to make camp, and had not bothered to pick it up again in the morning, finding it more pleasant to choose his own way through the hills, aided by instinct and memory. Besides, after a certain number of attempts on his life, a man tended to become wary of streets, roads, and marked trails.

Riding along at an easy pace, he gave some thought to the various hostile acts committed against him recently. The only enemy whose motives seemed simple and comprehensible was Paul Westerman, an ambitious and ruthless man. Then there was Willie Black, in whom jealousy and an old hate were complicated by the self-righteous egotism of the reformed sinner. Then . . . but Cohoon carried the analysis no further. He did not want to spoil a pleasant morning by thinking of the Paradines, or old Van Houck, as possible enemies. There was an ugly pattern here, and it would become clear in due time; nothing would be gained by borrowing trouble in advance.

The morning was a fine one; there were clouds and perhaps rain over the Candelarias to the south, but here the sun was shining brightly in a cloudless sky. He took pleasure in riding along, self-sufficient and independent; he let his mind wander over the things to be done at the ranch. Spring was getting on; it was time to buckle down and get to work. The wild stock would have to be routed out of the breaks and canyons—after three years the cattle would be hard to drive, and branding them would be no picnic. Then it would be a matter of weeding out the old stuff and judging the quality of what was left.

His father had never paid much attention to cattle breeding, Cohoon reflected; to Ward Cohoon, a cow had been a cow. But even before he had gone to prison, Cohoon had heard and read of new strains being introduced farther east; well, if there was money enough to experiment, it would be interesting to

117

see just what kind of scientific beef could be raised in this territory. In any case, he thought wryly, there would be plenty of work to keep a man too busy for brooding over the past or wondering about the future. . . .

It was close to noon when a rise of ground gave him a glimpse of the bridge ahead. He debated stopping for lunch, but his eagerness to reach the Grant was suddenly strong; another hour and a half would bring him to Willow Spring, where there was both shade and water. He rode on, therefore, making his way down toward the river, and struck the road where it leveled off, after its winding course through the hill, to make a straight run for the bridge. The long and narrow span looked untrustworthy to Cohoon's eyes; he thought he could see it sway in the breeze up the canyon. He laughed at his own fears; if it would bear a stagecoach, it would certainly take a horse and rider. Nevertheless, as he rode out onto it, he had to admit that it made him more uneasy than he had ever been on Black's old ferry—still visible below at the foot of the switchback road down the south canyon wall.

There was a dizzy sensation to riding over empty space; the river below, sliding slick and yellow past the deserted ferry and its decaying landings, looked small and far away. John Black's heavy cable looked like a string down there. Cohoon was aware of the muted thunder of the rapids downstream; it had been in his ears for the past hour, but he had not thought about it before. Well, he reflected, if you dropped from this height the rapids would be nothing to worry about since the fall would undoubtedly kill you. . . . A sound made him turn in the saddle to look back. The end of the bridge that he had just left was blocked by a dozen riders. At the head of them was Willie Black, conspicuous in his neat, dark suit.

"You're under arrest, Cohoon!" the marshal shouted, his voice diluted by the sound of the river. "Give yourself up quietly and I'll guarantee you a fair trial."

Another voice shouted, "Yeh, a fair trial and a good stout rope!"

Cohoon lifted his reins. The marshal saw the gesture and raised his gun to fire once in the air. "You can't get away," he called to Cohoon. "We've got you boxed."

He pointed ahead, and Cohoon turned to see another group of riders come around the bend in the road a quarter of a mile ahead, riding in to block the south end of the bridge in response to Black's signal. There was no time to waste in wondering what these men thought he had done that deserved hanging; and it was clear they were in no mood to listen to denials. Cohoon drove the spurs in hard. At least he could reach a better place to make a stand than this one, suspended over five hundred feet of nothing.

The men ahead, seeing his action, raised a yell and came rushing down the road, racing him for the end of the bridge; but he had much the shorter distance to go. The hollow thunder of his progress changed to a hard chopping sound as he reached solid ground; a bullet went by on a sharp, whining note, and he heard guns firing behind him, but did not look back, keeping his attention on the group charging down on him from ahead.

There were too many for him to have a chance of breaking through, and the men from behind were coming up fast. He knew a moment of rage and hatred more bitter than he had ever experienced. The impulse to stop, dismount, and, shooting carefully, take as many with him as he could, was very strong. With his father's old Henry he could make a shambles of that heedlessly charging mob in the minutes or seconds before one of their bullets found him. But into his mind came the sound of Ward Cohoon's voice, saying, *A man can always find a place to die; the trick is to find a place to keep on living.*

He reined the horse around sharply and spurred hard; the beast shuddered, and lunged desperately at the steep bank to the right. A bullet touched Cohoon's sleeve and another kicked up dust beside him as he crouched over the saddle horn, throwing his weight forward to help the laboring animal. Behind and below him the two halves of the posse came together and began milling in confusion. They had expected him to make his try toward the open country to the east, and had fanned out to block escape in that direction. But there was no escape to the west, where a sheer red bluff made progress downstream impossible except by a detour of several miles—Cohoon heard Black's voice ordering a handful of men, by name, to cut south and keep him penned into the open rectangle formed by the bluff, the canyon, and the road.

He was still boxed, he reflected grimly; but there was a hole in the box—although it was a hole no sane man would try to use. Well, a man who would spend five years in prison on the strength of a girl's smile could hardly be considered to have full possession of his senses. . . . Bullets were still pecking at the ground around him; then the tiring horse lurched over the crest of the slope, and Cohoon sent it forward at a run, angling back toward the river, to the bewilderment of the half-dozen riders who came into sight a moment later. Seeing him merely riding deeper into the trap in which they held him, they reined in and took time to organize the next phase of the campaign, and wait for reinforcements, allowing Cohoon to reach the canyon rim unhindered.

He followed the rim downstream, sparing the horse now that he had a little time; presently, in the shadow of the bluff, he came upon the old road that had carried traffic down to the river during the years John Black's ferry had been in operation under the guidance of the old scoundrel himself or his son—thinking this, Cohoon heard Willie Black's voice shouting crisp orders behind him. They were drawing up a cordon now across the angle formed by the river and the bluff. Willie's dad would turn over in his grave, Cohoon reflected wryly, to see his boy wearing a star. He turned the horse along the deep old tracks, blurred now with disuse, and rode over the edge onto the first of the switchbacks leading down to the water.

From here he could again see the bridge. It held a handful of men, dismounted. Seeing him come into sight, they began to shoot at him, but their weapons and marksmanship left something to be desired at five hundred yards Also, their hearts were clearly not in it: he was theirs, there was no place for him to go, and they preferred to enjoy his fruitless struggles for a while longer. Nevertheless, the sporadic reports of the guns, and the occasional whine of a bullet, made the precipitous, constantly reversing road seem considerably longer than he remembered it. He was halfway down when a rider came out of the hills to the north and charged across the bridge at a labored gallop—even at this distance it was clear that the horse was almost finished. Cohoon had a moment's hope that this might be a messenger from town to tell the posse they were making a mistake, but the shooting did not stop.

He negotiated a washout; the road was easier below, and he reached the bottom without further incident, dismounted, and got his rifle and his rope. Then he approached the deserted ferry. He had to wade to reach it, which was all to the good; high and dry it would have been useless to him. He threw his belongings aboard and, after a moment's study, put his shoulder against the sloping front of the scow and heaved strongly at the angle that seemed most promising. He was aware that men had reached the canyon rim above him now; there seemed to be some sort of an argument in progress, since they were all gathered in a bunch talking instead of shooting or coming down to get him.

He pushed hard, feeling his muscles crack and his boots drive into the yellow mud of the riverbank with the strain.

But it seemed that John Black's ferry, having made its last official trip, was not eager to come out of retirement. There were men riding back across the bridge now, heading for the old road leading down the north wall to the other landing, to meet him if he should succeed in making the crossing. Cohoon grinned tightly at this, drew a deep breath, and called upon all his strength; above the ever-present sound of the river, he heard a small sucking noise. Somewhere the mud was losing its grip on the waterlogged boards. Fearful of losing what he had gained, he continued to shove from the same position despite the fact that his feet were beginning to slide in the slippery mud.

A bullet hit the water nearby. Shouts and the sound of gunfire reached him from above; apparently the argument up there had ended. Cohoon took a fresh purchase, but he was tiring now, and could not start the sluggish craft again. Then running feet splashed through the water nearby, and he looked around quickly, reaching for the revolver at his belt—and stopped the motion, staring at Claire Paradine as she waded toward him heedlessly.

"They wouldn't believe me!" she cried. "I told them that I'd lied—that they had made me lie—but they laughed at me. Boyd, what can I do?"

He came out of his momentary paralysis. "Go back," he said. "This is no place for you."

"Don't send me away," she gasped. "Please don't send me away! Let me help."

He hesitated, and glanced at the road down which she had come; men were already following her down. He looked at her a moment; then he shrugged. He had protected her once. Remembering the payment it had earned him, he could not see doing it again. She was old enough to know her own mind.

"If you wish," he said. "Let's see if we can get this thing afloat."

"But—"

"Did you come to help or talk?" he asked harshly, not fully understanding her presence, and as deeply disturbed by it as the moment would permit. He threw himself against the weathered boards with sudden anger, and she came to push beside him. It was nothing like the picture he had carried of her through the years; he could never have imagined Claire Paradine knee-deep in muddy water, laboring like a squaw beside him—yet it gave him strength, and the scow began to slide as they pushed together. Suddenly it was riding free, swinging

121

slightly to the current. Cohoon caught the girl by the arm.

"Last chance," he said. "Go back, Claire."

She looked up at him, and shook her head stubbornly. He hauled himself aboard and reached down for her, telling himself that he could not leave her to the mercy of the mob—and knowing quite well that he wanted her with him. Yet it was, he knew, a vengeful kind of wanting, of which he was ashamed: she had refused to come with him once when coming might have been easy; it seemed like retribution that she should accompany him now, when it was hard. But there was no time to undo what had been done. She was aboard, and the ferry was already sliding smoothly away from shore, driven by the pressure of the current down the curve of the cable that would carry them as far as midstream.

Cohoon rose, and picked up the single, long, weatherbeaten sweep that John Black had kept aboard as a feeble gesture toward a possible emergency, but there was no need for it. The current kept them moving. Claire tossed the long, loose, disheveled fair hair back from her face and looked up.

"I betrayed you twice, Boyd," she said. "Once that you don't even know about. Does this make up for it?"

He grinned abruptly, "Honey, you shouldn't make it sound so damn much like a duty."

She rose, and pulled at her wet skirts, and glanced around. "Have we got away from them. . . . Oh, no! Boyd, they're on the other shore waiting for us! What are we going to do?"

The ferry came to a deliberate halt in the center of its arc; from here it was uphill work to the other shore, if you wanted to go there. Cohoon looked briefly at the girl beside him. He laid down the sweep and picked up the rifle instead, levered a shell into the chamber, and aimed the weapon carefully. Realizing his intention at last, Claire cried out in panic:

"No, Boyd, no! We'll be killed!"

The gun fired. The bullet tore through the heart of John Black's ancient cable. For a moment nothing happened; then the wounded strands began to separate and unravel, stretching unbelievably and parting with slow reluctance. . . .

The lurch as the cable gave way threw both occupants of the ferry to the deck. Free, for the first time in its long life, John Black's ferry seemed to hesitate for an instant before it began to slide downstream toward the first of the roaring rapids between this point and Yellow Ford.

23

NAN MONTOYA drew the green riding habit from the trunk with stiff fingers, not knowing exactly what she planned to do, only that she could not sit here, inactive and helpless, after the news she had just heard.

"He took the damn old scow into the middle of the river," the man had said, pausing on his way into Flagler's to make the announcement. "Took her right out into the middle and shot the cable in two. The Paradine girl went with him. Well, if they'd rather have the river than a rope, I reckon the choice was theirs. Who'll buy me a drink?"

Nan laid the garments on the bed, and began to unbutton the gingham dress she was wearing. A shocked word of protest sounded behind her; and Jesusa marched past her and gathered up the riding habit, exclaiming over its creased condition in voluble Spanish, and bearing it out into the other room to be ironed. Annoyed, Nan started after the old woman, but checked herself. After a moment, she fastened up her dress again mechanically, and walked quickly out of the house by the back door—it had been a fantastic idea anyway, born of despair. What could she accomplish down by the river by herself?

The sun was hot on her shoulders and bare head; she could feel the heat of the ground through her shoes. The wind scorched her face and the dust stung her eyes. It was a grim and merciless country, she thought; there had been a time when it had interested and challenged her, when she had dreamed of defeating it and the people it contained, but that time was gone. Suddenly she seemed to have no strength or will to fight. *I should have gone home with Lawrence*, she thought bleakly, *it would have been better than this, better than being alone.*

A murmur of voices caught her attention. She heard the clatter of many horses coming up Main Street and realized that the main body of the posse was returning, and that the town had come out to meet it. Already, when she reached the corner of Creek Lane, there were fifty people gathered around the dusty, sweating men as they dismounted. She saw that some did not stop here but rode on, meeting nobody's eyes; they would be the ones who felt the death of a woman on their consciences. The rest, however, were ready enough to share their experiences with anyone who would pay for the drinks.

Nan found herself trembling; hidden in the crowd, she crouched slightly, reaching down. Montoya's little gun was a weight at her knee; for a moment she was ready to snatch it out and empty it into any one of those gloating, triumphant faces. Common sense intervened, and she straightened up, and turned sharply away, needing to escape to some dark and private place. . . .

"Miss Montoya."

She recognized the voice and swung around. "*Mrs.* Montoya, Marshal," she whispered, looking into the face of William Black. The thought of the gun returned to her mind; and she knew surprise. Even during the recent, bitter years she had never hated anyone enough to kill; but she knew that she could kill this man without a qualm.

"I'm sorry." Black's voice was even. "*Mrs.* Montoya. I would like to talk to you, ma'am."

"You'd better go," she said. "I'm thinking of killing you and I have a gun. Get out of my sight, Marshal, before I forget that your death will do no good."

"Please, ma'am. There's something I'd like to ask. . . ."

He was quite young, she realized in sudden surprise; he sounded like a polite schoolboy asking a favor, and she looked into his face more closely, and was startled at what she saw. This was a different man from the arrogant officer of the law who had invaded her house that morning; now his face was set in grim lines, and his eyes had a blind look of suffering.

She heard herself say, "Ask your question."

The crowd had drifted away from them a little; they had space to themselves. The marshal licked his lips. "Mrs. Montoya," he said, "Mrs. Montoya, was I wrong?"

After a moment, she nodded. "Yes. You were wrong."

"Can you prove it?"

"What good will it do, now?" She shrugged. "I told you about the knife. Did you check on that?"

"No."

"Do so. You'll find I'm telling the truth. As for the identification—"

Black said softly, "Miss Paradine retracted her identification. At the river. The men . . . the men did not believe her."

"What more do you need?"

"The money," Black said. "The money from the first rob-

124

bery. The money you deposited in the bank the following day. . . ."

She shook her head. "You're barking up the wrong tree. That money was given to Cohoon by the Paradines, for services rendered. If you've heard the gossip of the town, you know what services I mean."

"I heard some stories, but I never believed them. It was not in the character of any Cohoon to make such a gesture."

Nan cried angrily, "What do you know of his character? All you know is that his brother played a cruel trick on you once; for that, you've hounded Boyd and killed him!"

"She went with him," the marshal said dully. "I tried to hold her, but she broke away and rode down to join him—"

Nan said, "You're not interested in justice, Mr. Black, or in the fact that you sent an innocent man to his death. All that bothers you is that Claire Paradine became involved as well."

He looked up, startled; then he nodded slowly. "Perhaps you're right, ma'am. In that case . . . in that case, I have no business wearing this any longer, do I?" With an abrupt gesture he ripped the badge from his shirt and hurled it away from him, turning to stride away.

"Marshal," she called. "Mr. Black."

He paused. "What is it?"

"Is there any hope?"

He looked back. "My father used to boast about his exploits when he was drunk, Mrs. Montoya. Doubtless you've heard rumors; well they're all quite true. In all, he claimed to have sent eleven men down the river. Many were alive when they hit the water. None ever showed up at Yellow Ford, alive or dead. There are records of six others who, not having the money to pay the ferry charges, tried to swim across and failed. None were heard of again." Black paused, and went on. "I sent some men to Yellow Ford this morning, on the strength of the information you gave me—not that I believed it. If anyone gets through, those men will be waiting."

"Yes," she said bitterly, "with a rope."

Black gave her a strange, blank look, and walked away. She watched him out of sight. Presently she became aware of a drunken voice by the nearest saloon explaining in detail how the trap had been set at the bridge, and how Cohoon had ridden into it unsuspectingly. . . . Nan shivered and turned away, but checked herself at the sight of a well-dressed man of less than medium height who stood listening to the recital without expression—standing a little apart from the crowd as if, like most small men, he disliked being jostled.

She knew him by sight and reputation, of course: this was Paul Westerman who, once a Creek Lane gambler, had managed to build upon his winnings until he was rumored to own half the town and wield influence throughout the territory. This was the man who hated Cohoon and was to have married Claire Paradine. His feelings, Nan reflected, must be divided at this moment; it was no wonder he chose to conceal them. As she looked at him curiously, a large bearded man she had seen before came walking through the crowd in a casual way and paused beside the smaller man briefly, as if by accident; but a word was passed, and Nan saw the wicked light that flared for an instant in Westerman's eyes.

Then the bearded man moved on—his name was Jack Rudy, she recalled now—and Westerman, having regained his composure, held his place for some minutes longer. When he moved away, it was with the leisurely gait of a man who had lost interest in the proceedings. Nan hesitated, and found herself walking slowly after him.

She was remembering her discussion with Cohoon the night before—already it seemed years ago—and her own insistence that the man who called himself the General was someone well known in town. Whoever he was, he had set the mob on Cohoon's trail to draw public attention from his own crimes—and it could easily be the short, assured man walking ahead of her. If this were true, it would explain how he had so quickly grown in wealth and influence in the community. The profits from the General's robberies seemed a more likely source for the money that had financed his ambitious schemes than the winnings of a few lucky nights at poker. . . .

Evening was closing in on the town and the desert; the lengthening shadows made concealment easy. It did not, apparently, occur to Paul Westerman that he might be followed; he led her directly down Creek Lane to its end at the arroyo; then made his way to the right some hundred years to an adobe house that had been deserted for the obvious reason that a change in the course of the stream bed during a past flood had undermined and carried away the whole rear of the building, leaving the front half perched precariously on the edge of the ten-foot bank, wide open to the desert to the north, but still presenting a closed, civilized face toward the town.

Standing in the shadow of a nearby hut, Nan watched the small man ahead of her walk directly to this remnant of a dwelling and swing himself around the broken wall where it ended at the sheer edge of the bank, disappearing inside. After a reasonable delay to make sure he was not coming out

126

again immediately, she darted across the open space and crouched beneath a window, feeling a little ridiculous at behaving in such a stealthy manner. But the sound of voices acted as an effective antidote to her selfconsciousness; she found herself listening intently.

Westerman's voice said sharply, "You still haven't told me what you're doing here in that getup! Do you want to get yourself hanged?"

"Señor," said a slurred voice that was faintly familiar, "I am getting drunk, can't you see? For years I have pretended to be a worthless *borracho*. Who pays attention to the movements of a young man so obviously interested in nothing but whisky and women and more whisky? Today I am celebrating; for a change I am really getting drunk—"

"Well, get out of that costume and get drunk somewhere else before you get us all in trouble!" Westerman snapped.

The other laughed. "It's too late for that, *amigo*. You *are* in trouble. You will never use my father's bank for your clever schemes, because I smashed it this morning, and him with it. You'll never marry my sister for the respectability she would bring you. . . . You wanted to marry into the fine Paradine family and move into the fine Paradine house; but what you didn't know was that it was a house of cards. Well, I blew it over today, *amigo*, with one little puff of breath. Poof, like that. So much for the Paradines, and so much for you, Westerman. You've been playing a game with me for years, ever since you learned the General's identity, using me as a weapon to terrorize this country, and taking half the profits for yourself. You were waiting, weren't you, for the right moment to take your revenge for Harry—oh, you know what I mean, and I know you know. But I was playing a game with you, too, my friend; and I struck first. And now I'll tell you this: your Harry was a yellow rat. The only courage he had was in his trigger finger. I warned him once that I would leave him to his own devices if he could not keep his nerves under control. Well, he lost his head again and started shooting, as was his habit, and I kept my promise and rode out on him. That's how Harry died, Westerman, a trigger-happy little coward. . . ."

There was a rustle of movement, and the sound of a blow. It was time to go for help, and Nan started up—and froze, seeing Jack Rudy watching her from the corner of the derelict house, a sly grin on his bearded lips. He stepped forward. She ducked, and reached for the gun she carried; but his powerful arm clamped about her, pinning her own arms to her body. The gun fell to the ground. She kicked hard, driving backwards with her heel; the man holding her swore in an ugly fashion, and his fist caught her behind the ear. Through the mists of receding consciousness she became aware that hers had not been the only struggle; inside the half-shell of a house, another human being was fighting for life against odds. But that resistance, also, was almost at an end.

24

THE SCOW HAD STRUCK once in the first rapids—struck, and hung on the submerged ledge for an interminable time, while the roaring water beat against it and washed over it; then it had pivoted in a deliberate way and, grindingly, pulled free to be flung out by the current into the smooth run of water below, down which it slid with frightening speed, rotating slowly. Cohoon released the girl and rose, aware that the craft beneath him, already waterlogged at the start of the journey, was settling more rapidly now as the water reached cracks opened by long exposure to the hot sun and dry air.

"Give me your shoes," he said to Claire.

She looked at him blankly through the matted veil of hair that had washed over her face. He was aware of regret and a sense of guilt; whatever she had done to him, he had his revenge in full, and it was a tasteless thing. He crouched beside her and removed her shoes, and his boots, and lashed these, with the rifle, to the weatherbeaten sweep lying on deck. He left two loops of rope lying free. The girl watched numbly; all hope and interest had been knocked out of her by the recent buffeting, as well as by her conviction that they were doomed.

He tried to encourage her, shouting over the roar of the next rapids, now close at hand, "As Father used to say, there never was a horse that couldn't be rode, or a river that couldn't be run. If we can just get down to where the canyon opens up a bit. . . . Hang on, now. Here we go again."

The ancient ferry seemed to pause; it tilted and plunged down a foaming chute into black shadows. Here the canyon walls were perpendicular and so high as to shut out the light of the afternoon sun. In the shadows, the current was torn apart by hidden rocks; they hit three times before they were borne out into sunlight again. Cohoon, lying on the deck beside the girl, took advantage of the respite to drag the sweep closer, and fit the rope about them; then they were thrown against the shore rocks with a splintering crash, and borne away, and hurled down a long incline of white water, in the middle of which the scow, riding deep now, struck with an impact that sent them sliding across the deck. It hung there; slowly the upstream side began to rise under the terrible pressure; boards and timbers cracked below. The deck began to open up; the whole fabric of the craft was dissolving.

There was no need to jump; the lower side was already submerged, and the angle of the deck let them slide into the water merely by letting to, but Cohoon had to break the girl's fingers loose from the panicky grips they found. Then they were floating free, still in the shelter formed by the grounded ferry. A moment later the current snatched them away.

Cohoon could never clearly recall the rest of that journey. He remembered seeing, behind them, the ferry upended and overturned and hurled like a toy after them, only to strike again and disintegrate into a mass of broken lumber. He had a memory of releasing the gun and belt that weighed him down. He remembered also, once when an eddy threw them close to the shore, that Claire had come suddenly to life and tried to free herself from the ropes to swim to safety; he had to grab her and hold her. There was nothing to be gained by reaching shore here, only to die of starvation under these towering red cliffs. Sunlight alternated with shade as they were implacably carried along; smooth water with rough. Claire lost consciousness, and he did his best to keep her head above water. Then a run of swift water shot them out into sunlight again, and the canyon walls were not as close as they had been, and he knew that this was the place for which he had been waiting, saving his strength.

He changed his grip on the sweep and, kicking hard, tried to drive them toward the south bank that was sliding past with frightening speed. Ahead the canyon narrowed again to a dark gateway beyond which more rapids roared. They had come less than a quarter of the way; they could never survive the rest. Even dead men had never made the full journey. . . . He labored desperately, and an eddy flung them back; he had to rest for a moment, and another eddy bore them shorewards, and he rode it in and fought blindly and furiously against the grip of it as it threatened to carry them out again. He broke free, and lay panting in a quiet backwater, floating on the sweep. Straightening, he felt his feet touch bottom.

Later he dragged the girl, and the sweep with its attached burden, up the clay beach. He determined that Claire was alive; and started for the oar with some notion of breaking it up and using the fragments to make a fire to warm her, but dizziness hit him suddenly, and he had to lie down. Lying there, he fell asleep. When he awoke, there was darkness all around him, but there was light in the sky upstream, which confused him, since it was his understanding that the sun normally set in the west. Then he laughed, realizing that he had slept the night through and this was morning.

He rose, limped back and forth a couple of times to loosen his abused muscles, and set to work to build the fire he had intended to make the evening before, using matches from the waterproof cache he always carried—even with this, he had to strike three before finding one that would light. As the flames grew, he became aware of being watched, and turned to see Claire's eyes open.

"What time is it?" she asked.

It seemed like an odd question, but he did not comment on it, answering: "I don't rightly know. Morning, anyway."

She sat up, and cried out. He went to her and helped her rise. "Oh, I feel like I'd been broken into a thousand pieces!" she whimpered. "Boyd, where are we? What are we going to do? How are we going to get out of this terrible place?"

"Walk," he said.

She glanced at him quickly.

He said, "Don't you remember, Claire. We climbed down here once when we were kids."

She looked around. "It's dark," she said. "I didn't recognize. . . ." She turned back to him. "You kissed me," she said. "I remember that. It was the first time. You were kind of slow in getting around to it, Boyd."

She looked quickly away again, raised her hands to her hair and presently turned aside to bring her dress into as much order as its condition would permit; finished, she found her shoes and put them on. She returned to stand by the fire and spread her skirts, still heavy with moisture, to the warmth. She spoke again to Cohoon, who had used the interval for much the same purposes.

"Aren't you going to ask me any questions? Aren't you even curious why those men were trying to hang you?"

He grinned. "Right now, I'm just happy to be alive, ma'am."

"It was my fault," she said. "But I've paid for it, haven't I? Boyd, look at me? Tell me you don't hate me! Please!"

"I never did, Claire," he said, and added honestly, "except maybe a little, now and then. After dreaming for five years, a

130

man kind of hates to wake up and find he has nothing but the dream for his pains."

"I know," she said, "I know! It was unforgivable of me, but I was afraid; afraid you'd changed; afraid you wouldn't . . . wouldn't have anything left for us to live on; afraid of what Paul might do. . . ." Her voice died. She raised her head to look at him across the fire. "I'm not afraid any longer, Boyd."

He returned her look; after a moment he moved, circling the fire to go to her. She waited for him; when he reached her, she turned her face up for the kiss as she had once before, on his first night home, but this time her arms came tight about his neck and her body was soft and yielding beneath his hands. . . . They stood thus for a measurable period of time. Then her arms dropped away; and he stepped back. A long time passed, and the thunder of the river was all around them. She was the first to make a sound; she laughed sharply.

"It's funny, isn't it," she whispered. "We were so much in love; and now there's nothing left. Did you know?"

He shook his head.

"Neither did I," she breathed. "I thought . . . When did it happen, my dear? Was it during the years you were away; or did I kill it a few days ago? . . . Never mind. It doesn't matter. Boyd—"

"Yes?" he said.

"I'm still a woman," she said, facing him. "I'm yours if you want me. It's a need men have, isn't it, even without love? I can fill it as well as that creature on Creek Lane; the one who wouldn't lift a finger to help you yesterday. I have followed you into this place; I'm yours. At least one Paradine will pay what is owed."

He said stiffly, "You're paying a debt, Claire? Is that why you came?"

She moved her shoulders beneath the damp, soiled dress.

"Maybe I thought there might be more. Maybe I hoped . . . But it doesn't matter, and there has been too much cheating. I'll keep the bargain I made with you five years ago. I promised you something then, and it's yours for the taking—here and now if you wish. You can marry me later or not as you please. I can't be particular about that, can I—the sister of a wanted outlaw and the daughter of a thief?"

He did not understand the reference; but it was not the time to ask. He was shocked and embarrassed by what she was offering—and by the fact that he had no desire at all to accept the offer, even if it had not been unthinkable that he should so

131

take advantage of her weariness and dependence upon him in this place.

"Claire," he said, "Claire. . . ."

Then she was in his arms, crying bitterly; and he held her until the paroxysms subsided, and lent her a damp handkerchief with which to dry her eyes. She laughed suddenly, looking up at him.

"Well, at least I tried, my dear. The offer was made in good faith, and I do not withdraw it."

He said curtly, "It's getting light. We'd better be moving. It's going to be a hot day for climbing."

25

TOWARD NOON they stopped to rest, for the fifth time in an hour. Shade was becoming hard to find, even in the crevice up which they were now making their way, but when they sat back against the wall, the sun could not quite reach them. Sitting there, Cohoon inspected his rope and coiled it carefully. A rope was not much assistance to a man climbing upward; however it had served to help him pull the girl after him up the more difficult places. He laid the rope aside and picked up the rifle, which he had earlier cleaned and dried to the best of his ability.

He turned to Claire Paradine, lying back against the sandstone wall with her eyes closed. Her small face was dirty and her lips had a parched look. She had had no strength to spare for saving her clothing during the climb; and her light garments, already stained and yellowed by the sediment-laden waters of the river, were further discolored now by dust and perspiration, and damaged beyond hope of repair. She had the look, Cohoon thought, of a flower cruelly broken and trampled into the dirt—but behind his sympathy was a faint sense of irritation at her helplessness. It occurred to him that she had required—demanded, even—almost as much assistance the last time they had come this way. But he had taken pleasure in being allowed to help her then, and considered her brave just to make the venture. . . .

"Come on, Claire," he said gently, "it's only a little way to the top now."

"You said that two hours ago." She opened her eyes. "Leave

me here, Boyd. I'm only a burden to you. Just leave me; it's what I deserve."

This was the new and humble Claire Paradine, purged and purified by suffering, and rather proud of it. Cohoon had no sympathy with her attitude; he lifted her to her feet, picked up rope and rifle, and led her away. An hour later he hauled himself over the crumbling edge of the rimrock, reached down for the gun she passed him, and then caught her wrists and pulled her up beside him. They stood there for a while, hearing the muted rumble of the river below and behind them; ahead was the broad expanse of the Grant.

Cohoon said, "Well, we've still got about seven miles to water. Might as well start walking—"

"Boyd, look!"

He followed the direction of her pointing arm, and saw a bunch of horsemen coming down the side of a small knoll that overlooked the surrounding country, heading directly for them.

He said dryly, "You've got to hand it to Willie. He gets around. Looks like we've had all our trouble for nothing."

"You think it's the marshal?"

"Or Westerman's outfit. Either way they're not apt to be friendly." He sighed, and looked at the Henry rifle with the spliced stock. Deliberately he levered a shell into the empty chamber. "Maybe I should have done my shooting yesterday," he said, "when I had dry cartridges to shoot with. I don't even know if these are going to fire. Walk off to the left a way, Claire—"

"I won't leave you!"

He glanced at her. "Go on," he said. "I appreciate the sentiment, but it will do no good. There's only one rifle, anyway—" He checked himself, suddenly frowning as he regarded the approaching figures. "Why, that's just one rider and two led horses!" he said softly. "Why do you reckon a man would bring two saddled horses. . . ."

He saw the quick hope in Claire's eyes. He lowered the gun he held, and they stood side by side on the rim watching the unknown horseman come closer, until his neat and sober clothing was clearly visible. Cohoon stood motionless, but his thumb found the hammer of the rifle that he had let down when he lowered the weapon. The rider approached at an easy trot.

"That's far enough, Willie," Cohoon said presently.

Fifty yards away, Black reined in. "I've got water," he said. "Looks like you might find a use for it. There's food in the packs." Sitting there, he reached down slowly and unbuckled his gunbelt, removed it from his waist, buckled it again, and hung it on the saddle horn. Then, still moving with careful deliberation, he dismounted, and stepped away from the horse. "I'm unarmed, Cohoon," he said. "No gun. And no badge. I owe you an apology. I made a bad mistake yesterday, because of my dislike for you. I . . . I was afraid it was irretrievable; but I made a search along the river anyway, in the hope of being able to make amends."

Cohoon studied him for a moment, then shrugged, walked forward, took the water bottle from the saddle, and brought it to the girl, who drank greedily. Presently she looked up, almost guiltily, and passed the canteen back.

Cohoon said, "Hell of a country. One minute you're drowning; the next you're dying of thirst." He took a mouthful of water and washed it around with his tongue before swallowing. "Maybe that's what makes it interesting," he murmured.

"I have some news for Miss Paradine," Black said. "Bad news, I'm afraid."

Cohoon nodded. "I'll go make a fire," he said, and walked away.

From a distance, gathering wood, he saw the two of them talking together; abruptly the girl buried her face in her hands. Black hesitated, and took a step forward, and reached out to steady and hold her as she cried. Cohoon grimaced at some unformed thought, and knelt down to set the wood alight, discarding two damp matches before he found one that would strike. When the fire was burning well, he went to the horses for food and utensils. The meal had been ready for some time when the two at last came over to join him. They did not explain their conversation to him, and he did not ask.

Presently Black rose to put away the remains of the food. When he was out of earshot, Claire spoke.

"He wants me to go with him, Boyd."

"Where?"

"Anywhere. Away. He made a mistake of trying to live down his father's reputation here. He's going somewhere where no one ever heard of John Black or Black's Ferry or . . . or the bodies slipped into the river in the dead of night. And I'm going with him, my dear. I can't go back to Sombrero, either. You'll learn the reason soon enough. I would have to spend the rest of my life living down the fact that I was a Paradine. . . ." She shook her head quickly, and looked toward the man by the horses. "We're the same kind, and we have the same problem. We'll get along together. Besides, he loves me."

"I wish you luck," Cohoon said.

"I know you do," she said. "I hope I'll deserve it. Goodby, Boyd."

Bill Black came back to them, carrying a paper-wrapped object which he gave to Cohoon. "You'll have no trouble in town," he said. "I found enough evidence, asking around, to straighten things out for you. Your friend Van Houck is taking care of it."

Cohoon watched them mount and ride away; then he unwrapped the thing in his hand, his father's knife, dull with dried blood. He cleaned it and replaced it in the sheath he still carried. The horse Black had provided looked adequate, but the saddle carried no rifle scabbard. Cohoon swung aboard holding the gun, and balanced it across the pommel as he rode. There was no longer any sign of the pair ahead of him except hoofprints in the dirt. Presently these swung left toward the main road. Rather than chance overtaking them, Cohoon turned west. He had said everything to those two that needed saying.

Riding along, he felt a little lonely; and he knew that even during the past few days he had been clinging desperately to the remnants of a dream, now lost for good. It was a long ride down the length of the Grant, but he welcomed the opportunity to put his thoughts in order. Presently it occurred to him to ask himself why he was riding to Sombrero at all; he had horse, rope, and gun here, and a mule-load of supplies was still cached near the burned ranch house. Furthermore, it might be well to let the situation in town cool for a day or two before riding in to face the men who only yesterday had been ready to put a rope about his neck. . . .

Nevertheless, he continued to ride westward until he reached the point where the old road came steeply up through the cliffs from Yellow Ford. Here he paused, studying the ground: a light wagon had come this way since his last visit to the ranch. He dismounted, and walked out on a point to look the situation over before descending. Even from this height, he could see that men had spent some time along the riverbank quite recently—part of Black's posse, no doubt, now recalled. One fire still sent a dying spiral of smoke into the sky, but the men were gone.

The ford was not quite deserted, however. A single horse grazed on the far bank, moving with the crabwise gait of an animal trailing its reins. There was, Cohoon thought, a saddle on its back, although it was hard to be sure at the distance. There was no sign of the rider.

Cohoon returned to his own horse, mounted, and proceeded down the steep road cautiously with his rifle ready. The river seemed strangely peaceful when he reached it; the rapids upstream made only a subdued murmur here. The grazing horse made no effort to avoid him. It bore a saddle, as he had thought—a fancy Mexican rig—and there was blood on the leather, some of it fresh enough to be tacky to the touch. Leading both animals, Cohoon began backtracking on foot. The trail did not lead far; there had been enough grass to keep the horse from wandering. He quickly found the spot where the rider had fallen.

There was dried blood in the dust; and the crippled marks left by a man crawling. He followed these, and came upon the man, who had found shelter in a shallow draw. The gaudy costume caught his eye first, although soiled and torn; then the wearer looked up, showing his face.

"I want no help from you, Cohoon," said Francis Paradine.

Claire had told enough of what had happened at the bank that the surprise was less than it might have been. Cohoon knelt without speaking. The boy had been badly beaten, apparently after being disarmed: his holsters were empty. His scalp had been laid open by a blow from behind, and his face was bruised and swollen. Cohoon could not help thinking that this was not the day for the Paradines—remembering the disheveled state in which he had last seen this boy's sister.

"Leave me alone," Francis whispered petulantly. "They finished it with a knife in the back; I'm done. Not your knife, Cohoon, another. I found good use for yours." There was malicious pleasure in his eyes and voice at the memory. "Too bad they didn't hang you. You might have found it harder to be a hero at the end of a rope than behind bars. Next time . . . next time you save a man from prison, Cohoon, ask him first if he wants to be saved!"

Cohoon asked, "Who did this?"

"Never mind. If I can't . . . settle with him myself . . . tried . . . couldn't make . . ." The boy's eyes closed, and opened again, bright and malevolent. "But whoever did it, robbed you, Cohoon."

"Robbed me? Of what?"

"Of vengeance." He smiled a terrible, bloodstained smile. "I shot your dad in the back, my friend. Why? Because he knew; he was the only one besides you and the family who *knew* who had ridden with Harry Westerman on the first, stupid holdup. He had taken care of me while I was wounded, remember?"

"You killed him for that?" Cohoon whispered incredulously.

Francis shook his head. "Not for that exactly. But, knowing, he guessed who was wearing the fancy uniform when the General began to operate on a larger scale; he challenged me with it. We met outside of town. He said that by God, if his boy thought enough of the Paradine family to go to jail to protect me, I was damn well going to stay protected; he wasn't going to have you save me from the consequences of one crime just to have me hanged for another. Rather than that, he'd spill the beans entirely. He had enough evidence, he said, to get you out of prison and me in. If the General pulled one more job, he said, he'd go to the authorities. . . ." The boy paused for breath, and went on calmly: "He laid down his ultimatum. When he rode away, I shot him. I knew Jonathan would be on my trail, so I rode to the ranch and took care of him, too, and set fire to the place in case your dad had thought to put anything in writing." Francis Paradine smiled. "It's a pleasure to tell you, Cohoon. To tell you and watch you sitting there gritting your teeth helplessly. What can you do to a dying man? But you're welcome to try. Hit me, shoot me, stick another knife in me; maybe it'll make you feel better. . . ."

Cohoon moistened his lips. "I'll get some water," he said, rising. Later, he could never remember whether it was a sound or merely instinct that made him glance around in time to see the little nickel-plated revolver pointing directly at him, as he reached for the water bottle on the saddle.

He threw himself aside, placing the horse between himself and the muzzle of the weapon. The animal reared at the first shot; the gun continued to discharge with a small, spiteful sound, but Cohoon was flat on the ground now, and the boy, lying in the sheltering depression, could not, apparently, find strength enough to push himself up to shoot over the edge; his bullets either hit the dirt bank harmlessly or whined off overhead.

Afterwards, the silence ran on interminably. When Cohoon raised himself at last to look down, Francis Paradine's eyes were closed, and the gun had fallen from his hand. Cohoon stepped into the wash, and started to kick the empty weapon aside, but the appearance of it caught his attention. He bent down and picked it up, examining it closely, with sudden apprehension. A slight movement made him glance at the boy, whose eyes had opened.

"Recognize it?" Francis Paradine whispered. "Yes, it's hers, Cohoon. That uppity wench of yours from Miss Bessie's; too

137

good to be friendly with the regular customers. She was snooping around the shack; she must have dropped it when they grabbed her. . . . They took my guns; it was all I could find. . . ." His lips continued to move, but no more sound came out.

Cohoon knelt beside him, and cried urgently: "Who has her, Paradine? Where's she been taken?"

Francis's eyes opened slowly. "Why, I'll be nice and tell you," he whispered. "Westerman has her, Cohoon, if she's still alive; or even if she isn't. Couldn't leave a witness to spread the news that he was the General's partner . . . in a wagon, heading for the mine, deep shafts, tons of rock, never a trace; who'll waste time hunting for a missing Creek Lane wench. . . . Go find her, Cohoon!" he breathed. "Go find her. And Westerman too. I wish I could see the two of you shoot it out. It would almost be worth . . ." He winced at some intolerable pain, but a hint of a smile remained. "I hope you shoot straight—both of you!"

26

THE MINE LOOKED small down in the rocky canyon; just a few weathered shacks and some battered machinery showed above ground. Cohoon rested his horse at the top of the pine ridge to the west, and studied the place carefully despite the urgency within him; presently he rode on up the ridge, gradually angling down the slope to the left, keeping in the shelter of the trees. At last he dismounted, tied the horse, and went forward on foot.

All of this country was in shadow now, but the sun still shone on the higher Candelaria peaks, making the bare granite glow with reddish light. The air was suddenly quite cool after the heat of the day. The smoke from the cookshack below rose straight into the evening sky. The cook was splitting wood by the door of the shabby structure. Cohoon watched the man sink his hatchet into the chopping block, gather up the split sticks, and disappear inside.

Off to the left, another man, his shirt removed to expose faded red underwear, was shaving by the aid of a mirror fastened to the outer wall of the bunk-house, presumably in preparation for a visit to town. Half a dozen others were rolling dice nearby, in the eager and careless fashion of men whose pay was heavy in their pockets. Cohoon recalled that the last payroll had been stolen; apparently the loss had been made good today by Westerman, providing an official reason for his visit.

It was a peaceful scene. Beside another flimsy frame cabin that probably served as an office—the name LUCKY SEVEN MINING CO. was painted on the board above the door—stood a light wagon. The team, unharnessed, grazed in a nearby corral with some mules and saddle stock. The wagon seemed quite empty except for a tarpaulin tossed into the bed of it. The heavy canvas took up a good deal of room, but no more, perhaps, than could be accounted for by its stiffness and the careless manner in which it had been stowed. . . . As Cohoon watched from the slope, a miner came around the corner of the building and paused by the vehicle; immediately Jack Rudy stepped out of the cabin door and spoke sharply. His words were inaudible at the distance, but his meaning was clear. The miner made an equally sharp retort, but moved on, pausing at a safe distance to look back at the wagon with obvious curiosity.

Cohoon forced himself to think clearly: *There's Rudy. Where's Westerman?* There was anger and fear and a sickening apprehension inside him; and he knew now what had drawn him toward town this afternoon, but this was no time for dramatic emotions. He watched Jack Rudy stand in the doorway forming a cigarette in a leisurely fasion; a large, bearded, confident man. Somebody spoke inside, and he answered, turned, and disappeared from sight. *Both of them inside,* Cohoon thought, *waiting for darkness. They would tell the miners it was money they were guarding, brought here for safekeeping from bandits, perhaps. Is she alive?* The question slipped into his mind unwanted, destroying the coolness he was trying to maintain; and suddenly he was running forward. A crevice let him down through a rocky rim to the talus slopes below, and he continued to the right at a lope, heading for a patch of mountain spruce that clung to the hillside ahead.

Reaching this, he pushed his way through and found himself lying in adequate cover within a hundred yards of the cook-shack, the office, and the wagon standing beside it. He forced himself to rest briefly, letting his whole body go slack until he had recovered somewhat from his exertions. When his breathing had returned nearly to normal, he pushed the rifle forward, and took careful aim at the nearest window of the building. He hesitated for a moment; there were better ways of doing this, but they would take more time, and he pressed the trigger. The weapon crashed, and the window shattered.

Jack Rudy came charging out, bull-like, rifle in hand. Cohoon waited.

The miners, startled by the shot, had drawn back; gun business was apparently none of their business. Presently, when no second shot followed the first, and Rudy remained unharmed where he stood in the open, Paul Westerman stepped warily through the doorway, holding a revolver ready.

Cohoon took careful aim. No one here deserved mercy, or even the favor of an even break; yet he found himself reluctant to press the trigger. In the moment that he hesitated, Westerman felt or saw something wrong and stepped back into shelter, crying a warning. Rudy dropped to one knee and fired into the trees; the bullet dropped a twig on Cohoon's head. The bearded man was levering a second shell into place when Cohoon caught him squarely in the sights of the old Henry. The cartridge fired, and Rudy rose to his feet, took three steps toward the corral, and fell heavily on top of his gun.

Westerman was shooting from the broken window. Cohoon put a bullet through the glass and another through the flimsy boards beside it; a sharp cry told him that either the bullet itself or a flying splinter had taken effect.

"Westerman!" he shouted. "This is Cohoon. Come out with your hands up and you'll live to stand trial. Don't make me smoke you out; this gun holds enough shells to make a sieve of that shack."

There was a brief silence; then Westerman's voice answered: "All right. Don't shoot. I'm coming out."

The small, important figure appeared in the doorway, arms raised. Westerman's face was bleeding. He moved forward in a docile enough manner, yet at an angle that did not bring him directly into the open, or toward Cohoon's hiding place. . . .

"Hold it right there!" Cohoon shouted.

Instantly Westerman threw himself aside, toward the wagon that was now within reach. As he lunged past the corner of the building, Cohoon saw him grasp for the butt of the revolver he had concealed beneath his belt at the small of his back. His intention was obvious: to use the wagon and its burden as a shield.

Cohoon swung the sights with—and slightly ahead of—that racing figure; then the barrel of the old Henry wavered oddly. He found himself losing control of the gun, for some reason he had no time to determine. It was too late, however, to check the movement of his trigger finger, and the piece fired wild. Instead of the recoil against his shoulder, he felt a sharp blow in the face, close enough to his eye to partially blind him for a moment or two.

Shaken and slightly dazed, Cohoon found himself holding a rifle that had separated into two pieces, the spliced stock having given away again under the repeated shock of recoil following the battering it had received in the river. He shook his head and found himself thinking that it was just as his father had always said: with a firearm, just about the time you got to depending on the thing, you found yourself in a spot where you couldn't use it because of the noise. Or you ran out of ammunition, or it broke down on you, or blew up. A knife or a tomahawk, now, or your bare hands, had none of those drawbacks. . . .

A hundred yards away, Westerman was kneeling in the wagon box, waiting for a target. He had thrown the tarpaulin aside and raised the cruelly bound and gagged figure of Nan Montoya before him as a shield. Cohoon rose deliberately to his feet and reached back for the knife; then he was running forward, weaving from side to side. Westerman awaited him calmly enough, saving his ammunition for a certain shot. Cohoon balanced the knife as he ran, knowing that the odds were against him here; the other could pick him off easily before he was close enough to make his throw good.

It occurred to him that his judgment seemed always to be at fault where this girl was concerned. Once, thinking she had betrayed him, he had unnecessarily tackled half a dozen men single-handed, too angry to retreat; now, seeing her limp and bound, he was charging foolishly into the muzzle of a loaded gun to save her. . . . The girl moved as Westerman fired, throwing the shot wild. There was a brief, uneven struggle in the wagon bed; Nan was flung aside, but she picked herself up to hurl her weight against Westerman as he shot again. The shot missed, but the girl's position forced Cohoon to deflect his throw at the last instant. The knife glinted harmlessly through the air, struck the side of the building, and fell to the ground.

Westerman laughed—a short bark of triumph—and rose from his knees to level the gun more accurately at his disarmed adversary. Nan rolled against him and he kicked at her viciously, and looked up to aim again. Then Cohoon, still running forward, had wrested the cook's hatchet from the block into which it had been sunk and, in the same motion, hurled it at the man on the wagon. Westerman saw the heavy weapon coming too late. It caught him in the shoulder and threw him back off the wagon box. For a moment he seemed to be leaning stiffly against the wall, then his body folded and slipped through the space between the wagon and the building, and lay there, quite still.

Cohoon ran forward; he was climbing into the wagon when the sound of many riders brought him around quickly, snatching up the revolver dropped by Westerman.

"Ach, there'll be no need for that, my boy," said Van Houck, coming around the corner of the building. "It's Westerman they want, not you. We have learned that he was the General's accomplice. . . . Conscience is a hard master, Boyd. I have worked hard for you this day. To avenge you, I thought. I'm glad it was not necessary. Aren't you going to help a tired old man off his horse?"

Cohoon grinned. "Fall off, you old fraud. Westerman's under the wagon. Excuse me, there's somebody who needs help worse than you do—and deserves it more, too."

27

She had not spoken for some time, riding beside him through the luminous night. He stopped at last, dismounted, and helped her down, steadying her.

"Are you all right?" he asked, suddenly concerned.

"It's a little late to ask," she said. "I died five miles back. Where in heaven's name are we?"

He pointed to a grove of trees below them, dark in the moonlight. "That's Willow Spring," he said. "Nan, what was in your mind when you sent Claire to warn me?"

She glanced at him quickly. "Sent? Did she say I sent her?"

"Far from it. But I say it."

She moved her shoulders in an abrupt manner. "Well, suppose I did. It was the logical thing. Being born and brought up here, she had a much better chance of finding you in time than I did." She paused; Cohoon did not speak. She asked, "Where is Claire now?"

"With Black. Riding south."

"You let her go?"

"There was no reason for her to stay. We learned that down there." He motioned toward where the distant canyon made a black pattern in the sloping plain below. "Did you know it when you sent her, Nan?"

She shook her head. "It was a chance. Perhaps I'm a gam-

142

ler at heart." After a moment she said, "I've had a hard day, Cohoon. I'm dirty and bruised, and I have rope-burns and saddle sores. So if you brought me here just to talk over old times—"

Cohoon said, "I would put the house up on this rise, although it means a longer walk for water. On a clear day, when the dust is not blowing, you can see Sombrero through a notch in the hills over there, thirty miles away."

"I've seen Sombrero," Nan said. "A woman likes a house with trees around it."

"I've asked you twice to marry me," he said. "I'm asking again. This time I'm free to ask."

"I know," she said, and seemed to be waiting.

He said, "I need you, Nan."

"Need?" she said. "Who cares about your needs, Cohoon?"

"I love you," he said, and she turned to him quickly, her waiting at an end.

Hard-Hitting...
Fast-Moving...
Action-Packed...

Donald Hamilton's
MATT HELM
SERIES